The last thing Sage Kanston wants to do is go to the Shifter Council Headquarters to help his older brother, Glade. He hadn't been on good terms with him . . . ever. While growing up, Sage remembered Glade to be a bully, and that trait hadn't changed when he'd been a pride enforcer. Sage doubted it had varied when he became a council enforcer, either. Still, he likes keeping his momma happy, so to the Council Headquarters he goes.

When the enforcer sent to escort Sage to Glade's boss arrives—some guy named Mycroft—he's hit with a scent he never expected. Germaine Messalla, the tall, slender, anaconda shifter, is his mate. His world is turned upside down because his pride always told him same-sex fated matings didn't happen. To make matters even more confusing, Sage learns that a couple of councilmen are in fated gay pairings. So many things he'd been taught . . . just aren't true.

As Sage comes to grips with the changes in his reality, allowing him to accept Germaine, he realizes others in his pride could benefit from what he's learned. Except, there are those attempting to keep the changes on the council secret. Can Sage and Germaine uncover who's still attempting to keep certain things under wraps so he can help his pride?

Snaking the Tiger
Copyright © 2021 Charlie Richards
ISBN: 978-1-4874-3201-0
Cover art by Angela Waters

Published by eXtasy Books Inc or
Devine Destinies, an imprint of eXtasy Books Inc

Look for us online at:
www.eXtasybooks.com or www.devinedestinies.com

SNAKING THE TIGER
SHIFTER'S REGIME BOOK SEVEN

BY

CHARLIE RICHARDS

DEDICATION

Common sense is like deodorant. The people who need it most
never use it.
~Anonymous

CHAPTER ONE

If Sage Kanston had been able to get out of it, he would have. Unfortunately, he liked having his mother happy with him. Especially when the action was fairly easy, just uncomfortable.

Mary Kanston was the only person in the pride who'd always encouraged him, even when she didn't understand his choices. Still, that didn't mean she didn't offer words of warning and discretion, too. It just meant they were wrapped up in motherly hugs and served with a cup of mint tea—her favorite.

To that end, Sage found himself making the twelve-hour drive to the outskirts of Savannah, Georgia and the building that housed Shifter Headquarters. To outsiders, it looked like an exclusive golf club and day spa. Paranormals knew differently—beneath the pretty window dressing above was a massive underground complex housing the Shifter Council's offices, suites in case they needed a place to rest and freshen up between meetings, plus cells, interrogation rooms, and sentencing chambers.

Sage's brother, Glade, had told him all about them. He'd made them sound terrifying. Sage never wanted to see them, since so few who went in as prisoners ever saw the light of day again.

Well, that's what Glade told me anyway. Maybe I shouldn't believe a word he says.

Except, Glade had scented true.

Being a tiger shifter—a paranormal that shared his psyche

1

with a Bengal tiger and could shift into the animal at will—
Sage could use a person's scent to tell if they were lying or
not. It wasn't an exact science, since if the person actually believed what they were saying, they would smell of truth.
Maybe Glade truly thought that was what happened to prisoners.

How ironic, then.

Sage couldn't help but smirk as the words flitted through
his mind. His brother was currently sitting in one of those
cells. According to what his father had told him, Glade had
allowed a rogue into the facility and had tried to help him
kidnap another enforcer's mate—some woman named
Miggs—while she'd been working in the headquarters'
kitchen.

Of course, then his father—Bill Kanston, their pride's head
enforcer—had made a snide comment about the woman's
name. "Who would name their daughter Miggs? Stupid
name," Bill had said. That was followed up by expressing his
bigotry. "At least she knows her place. In the kitchen."

Sage didn't know how his mother tolerated his dad's nar-
row-minded and controlling views. He supposed it had
something to do with the whole fated mate thing. In his opinion, Sage would rather never find his mate if it meant putting
up with that kind of attitude.

On top of that, Sage wouldn't know what to do with a
woman even if he did find his fated mate. He was as gay as
the day was long, not that he'd ever told his father that. His
mother knew, though. She'd told him she loved him just the
way he was, then followed that up by telling him, "But you
need to be very careful. Few people in the pride would understand, and I don't want you hurt or kicked out."

For over a century, Sage had taken that advice to heart.
He'd been extremely careful about who he'd shared his body
and time with. Over the last couple of decades, homosexuality

had become much more accepted — to humans, anyway. Paranormals were a bit slower to change. Perhaps it was due to their long lives. Still, it had made it easier for Sage to find lovers.

Hell, Sage even had a couple of friends-with-benefits in a fox skulk. Their territory abutted the pride's. Every month or so, he would go to his friends' home for a *movie night*. Randy and Cain weren't fated mates — after all, Fate didn't pair those of the same sex — but they were in a relationship. It was too bad, really, because the guys loved each other deeply.

Of course, if they had ended up fated mates, then they would never allow me to occasionally join them in their fun.

The movies they watched weren't of the normal variety. His buddies had an extensive porn collection, and Sage loved watching with them . . . which led to touching and so much more.

Just remembering the last Saturday night he'd spent with Randy and Cain caused his prick to begin to thicken. It had been the prior month, and the amount of fucking and being fucked he'd enjoyed had been fantastic. He clenched his chute as he recalled Cain's dick in his ass. Sage then remembered how it had felt to sink his cock into each of the men and had to adjust himself in his dress slacks.

Randy was a consummate bottom boy, but Cain enjoyed the occasional dick up his ass, too. Sage understood the man's position because he was a switch, too. He was only too happy to help both men scratch their itches.

Sage had regretfully had to tell Randy that he wouldn't be able to make it tomorrow evening, since he wouldn't be in town.

"You're going to Shifter Headquarters?" Randy had asked, sounding shocked. "To help *Glade*?"

"Afraid so," Sage had confirmed dryly, unable to hide his disappointment . . . or annoyance. "Not that I know what I'll be able to do, but my dad wants me to find out if the charges were just blown out of proportion. He says if family shows up to support him, maybe he'll get off."

"That sounds like bullshit," Cain commented, telling Sage that Randy must have put the phone on speaker. "If he really believes that, then why doesn't he go himself?"

Sage had cleared his throat, uncomfortable sharing pride and family secrets that weren't his, even with his friends. Still, he hadn't wanted to lie to the pair. "Well, my father checks emails before passing them on to Alpha Colton or Beta Larry, depending on which one he thinks would be better equipped to handle it."

"That's a lot of power for the head enforcer," Randy had murmured, sounding concerned. "Your alpha's okay with that?"

Cain's snort had come through the line before he'd claimed, "No way would Alpha Brenner be okay with that."

Sage had known Cain referenced their fox skulk's alpha. He'd had to meet the shifter once before getting permission to visit his friends on skulk land. He'd found the wiry shifter dominant and controlling, but not in an overbearing way. Alpha Brenner had asked Sage a few personal questions. Then he'd agreed that as long as Sage never started any trouble, he was welcome.

During their first movie night, as Sage had lain between Cain and Randy in their bed, their hands stroking over his chest, side, and spent cock, he'd asked if the alpha knew they weren't just friends—which was what Sage had told his own father.

Randy had chuckled softly and nodded. "Considering our scents are always all over each other, oh yeah, he knows."

"And he doesn't care?" Sage had been amazed.

Cain had shaken his head. "Alpha Brenner told us once that it's not hurting anyone in the skulk by us being together as long as we keep our private life behind closed doors," he'd murmured as he'd begun teasing his fingertips around and over Sage's nipple. "It means no making out in public, but we're not into that anyway."

Then Cain's lips had replaced his fingers on Sage's nipple, and there hadn't been much more talking that evening.

Occasionally, Sage recalled the conversation, and his gut churned with jealousy. He always pushed the sensation away. He'd never met a man that he'd been interested in sharing his home and life with the way Randy and Cain did, so there was no reason for the feeling.

Of course, that logical reasoning didn't keep him warm on cold, lonely, New England nights.

At least those thoughts brought Sage's arousal under control. No way did he want to show up at Shifter Headquarters sporting a boner. Talk about embarrassing.

Still, when he recalled Randy's pouting voice as he told him, "Well, me and Cain are gonna miss your big, beautiful dick Saturday." Humming, he'd added, "And maybe your gorgeous body, too."

Sage had chuckled, telling his friends, "And my dick will miss your asses and hands."

They'd laughed, and Sage had promised to let them know when he was home again.

"In a quarter-mile, turn left onto River View Drive."

The smooth tenor voice of Sage's navigational system pulled him out of his musings. He glanced at the map on his dash. Then he focused on the road and looked for his turn.

Sage found it and headed that way. As he peered around, he found the area lovely. Spring buds were beginning to sprout on the trees, and lush green grasses covered the ground. His tiger rumbled in the back of his mind, reminding him of how long it had been since he'd shifted. He liked to get his tiger out every three or four days, but his plan to shift had been derailed by his father ordering him to drive to Georgia.

It had been his mother's pleading expression that had him agreeing, however.

And all because my father doesn't want the alpha to know that his son is in the shifter jail.

It didn't help that his father had been angling to get Glade permission to court Alpha Colton's youngest daughter—Meribeth. She had recently turned twenty-seven, and Colton doted on her. Sage was pretty certain no one had figured out that she preferred her own sex, since Colton rarely allowed any guys near her. The only reason Sage suspected it was because he'd been out running once and spotted Meribeth and her good friend, Gwendolyn, in the garden once. The way Gwen had been petting Meribeth's shoulder and neck, coupled with the way the women had been smiling at each other, told Sage much more than what he figured they'd wanted anyone to see.

Sage had turned, intending to find a new direction to run in. Except, seeing Alpha Colton heading their way, he'd purposefully broken a branch under his paw. If their relationship was as he suspected, he hadn't wanted them to get caught.

Since Gwendolyn was still around and Meribeth hadn't been forced to wed some random male, Sage guessed her secret was still safe.

"Your destination is in one hundred yards on the left."

Sage shook his head, realizing he really needed to focus. Driving distracted was dangerous. As he turned into the driveway and stopped at the gate, he wondered if he should have stopped and gotten a hotel room first. It probably would have been wise to clean up.

Too late.

Leaning out the window, Sage pressed the *call* button.

"Yes?" a deep voice immediately responded.

"I'm Sage Kanston," Sage replied, speaking into the box. "I'm here to meet with Head Enforcer Mycroft Portent in regards to my brother, Glade Kanston."

Sage fought back a cringe, hating that he had to parley on behalf of a man who'd always been a bully to him, brother or not. Still, his mother had pleaded with her expression from over his father's shoulder. She didn't want her eldest to be punished or worse, not if something could be done about it. Seeing as Sage figured there was more to the story than what he'd been told about Glade's actions — his brother had always been an overbearing bully, but he'd also been a stickler for rules — he owed it to his mother to try to find out.

"Do you have an appointment?" the disembodied voice asked.

"Yes, sir," Sage replied respectfully.

"Just a moment."

Sage waited patiently, tipping his head back and enjoying the fresh afternoon air, which held just a touch of early-spring chill. The scents of flowers, trees, and grass filled his nostrils. Tipping his head to the side a little, Sage closed his eyes and just enjoyed the moment.

When Sage's tiger rumbled in his mind again, he smiled, mentally promising his animal that he would find a place to stretch their legs as soon as possible.

The rumble of the gate opening caused Sage to open his eyes.

"Take the right fork and enter the underground parking structure," the voice ordered. "Visitor parking is to your immediate left. Wait with your vehicle, and an enforcer will be there to escort you."

"Thank you, sir."

Sage wondered how serious Glade's crimes actually were that he would have to be escorted. As he pulled through the gate and followed the guard's directions, it occurred to him that maybe having an escort was standard procedure. The place was Shifter Headquarters, after all.

Going where ordered, Sage spotted the open bay door and

entered. He spotted a large parking area to the left. After he'd found a spot and turned off his *Wagoneer*, he still hadn't spotted anyone.

Taking advantage of the alone time, Sage slipped from his vehicle and stretched his arms over his head. He twisted his body this way and that, working the kinks out that had been caused by too many hours behind the wheel. Sage felt his back pop and sighed before lowering his arms.

"That sounded like it felt good."

Sage wheeled and spotted a tall, dark-skinned male leaning against the back corner of his vehicle. He stared at him with a predatory smile curving his lips and narrowed dark eyes that gleamed in the low lighting. His arms were crossed over his chest, but even in the semi-relaxed position, Sage would bet the handsome man could spring into action and take him down in a split second.

Mmmm. Take me down. What would that strong-looking, wiry body feel like pressed against mine?

Shit! Did I just think that? Stop that right now!

No way did Sage want to draw the wrong kind of attention from a Shifter Enforcer. Swallowing hard, he found ignoring the way his fingers practically tingled with his desire to rub his palms over the enforcer's pate, to see if it was as smooth as it looked surprisingly difficult. He did manage to get his tongue unstuck, however.

"Uh, yes, sir," Sage replied, answering the man's comment. "Long drive."

Tipping his head to the side just a little, the man inhaled deeply. His nostrils flared, and his smile stretched a bit. "That explains the intensity of your scent clinging to you."

His tone didn't make it sound as if he were put off by that, but Sage apologized anyway. "Uh, yeah. Sorry about that." Rubbing the back of his neck, he glanced around slowly, having trouble staring into the man's gaze without finding his body reacting to it. "Shoulda stopped at a hotel and showered."

"You misunderstand me," the man stated, pushing away from Sage's *Wagoneer*. "I like the way you smell." A roguish smile curved his lips as he began stalking forward. "You *are* my mate, after all." Holding out his hand, he claimed, "And I am Enforcer Germaine Messalla, anaconda shifter. What kind of kitty shifter are you, mate?"

Gaping, Sage reacted on instinct. Even as he shook Germaine's hand, the hairs on his arm standing on end from the tingles erupting from the contact, he muttered, "But Fate doesn't pair those of the same sex."

CHAPTER TWO

Germaine just resisted rolling his eyes. Instead, he tightened his grip on his mate's hand, refusing to allow him to pull away. "Really?" He eased even closer to the other shifter. "Then how would you explain the pull between us?"

The second Germaine had entered the parking garage, his snake had come alive in his mind. It had hissed in anticipation, and he'd obeyed his beast's mental command. Flicking out his tongue, he did something he rarely did.

He allowed his tongue to partially shift to his snake, giving him the ability to taste the air around him.

The flavor that had exploded across Germaine's senses had nearly dragged a moan from his chest. He'd spotted the shifter he'd thought he was to escort and headed his way. As he'd approached, he'd admired his compact body and leanly muscled frame. The way the shifter had twisted and turned, obviously stretching out some sort of sore muscles, had Germaine wondering how that flexibility would translate to bedplay.

Germaine had wanted to drag him into the car's backseat right then and there to find out. Considering the way the shifter immediately claimed they weren't mates, he figured that wouldn't have gone over well. He also silently vowed to change the man's misconception . . . and damn fast.

Even as the scent of the man's arousal perfumed the air, he replied, "Well, I'm gay, and you're hot."

The cat shifter swept his gaze over Germaine's frame slowly, down and up, and Germaine felt as if it were a physical caress. He desperately wanted to use the hold on the man's hand to tug him into his arms. He could press his mate's body flush to his own, and —

"And I figure, since you're coming onto me, and I smell your arousal, you're gay, too," the other shifter continued, dragging Germaine out of his thoughts. "So that means I won't get my ass kicked if I admit that."

Growling softly, Germaine rumbled, "Someone kicked your ass because you're gay?"

While clearing his throat, the shifter shook his head once. "No, but my momma warned me to be careful."

Sighing, Germaine eased closer. "First, I need to know your name."

As much as Germaine wanted to stand there and seduce his mate, he needed to know if he was the shifter he was supposed to escort. If he wasn't, then he needed to find the other guy. At the same time, he would request another enforcer be made available to take him to Mycroft.

"Sage Kanston," the shifter replied. He glanced at where Germaine continued to hold his hand while tugging lightly. "Um, is this appropriate?"

That solves one problem.

Germaine scented Sage's discomfort, and it took every bit of self-control he had to let the other shifter go. Needing to be close, he eased a step closer. Breathing deeply, he enjoyed another lungful of the cat shifter's delicious scent.

"Gods, you do smell wonderful, Sage," Germaine murmured, smiling down at the shorter man. Then something clicked. "Ah, so you're Glade's brother, and Glade thinks same-sex matings are not fated, either. Even though it's been proven time and time again that Fate really does sometimes pair two men or two women." With a wink, Germaine rested his hand on Sage's shoulder, slid his hand up a little, and teased his fingertips over the knobs of his spine below his nape. "Just like *you* are *my* mate, Sage." Seeing the hitch in Sage's breathing felt like a stroke to Germaine's ego. Even confused, his mate responded to his touch. "Do you really think Fate would give a gay shifter a female mate?" Letting out a light chuckle, Germaine added with a wink, "Whatever would you do with her?"

"Gods, that's the truth," Sage whispered breathily. Then his face flushed, and he cleared his throat. "You smell amazing, too."

"Thank you, Sage," Germaine all but purred. Easing even closer, he rested his other hand on Sage's hip. "So, we return to the problem of where your belief that Fate doesn't mate those of the same sex. Don't you know that a couple of the councilmen, as well as those working for the Shifter Council, have been gifted by Fate with a partner of the same sex?"

Sage's mouth opened, then closed. His brows furrowed, and he swallowed hard enough to cause his Adam's apple to bob. Finally, he squeaked, "Really?"

"Really," Germaine confirmed. Then he smiled as he admitted, "Do you have any idea how pleased I am that you already admit you're gay? You're out to your family, even if you didn't think a fated mate was possible." Germaine's heart thudded as he stared at the man's mouth. "And I really want to taste you."

"Yes, please."

Hearing Sage's softly spoken words, Germaine didn't wait a second longer. He tightened his hold on his mate's hip. At the same time, he slid his hand up to thread into Sage's hair.

Germaine pressed his lips to Sage's once, twice, before swiping his tongue along his bottom lip. His mate immediately opened, and he took complete advantage. Slipping his tongue into Sage's mouth, Germaine relished his first taste of the other man's masculine flavor.

Lapping at Sage's tongue, Germaine encouraged him to engage in the play with him. It only took a few seconds. Then Sage grabbed his waist and clung to him as he cocked his head and kissed him right back just as hard.

Growling lightly, Germaine spread his legs a little, lowering his stance. At the same time, he wrapped his arm around Sage's waist and tucked him against his leaner frame. The feel of his mate's body pressed against his own caused his blood to fire through his veins.

Holding Sage, Germaine reveled in the taste of his mate, in the way he slid his arms around his waist right back and clung. He even fed Germaine a few needy moans, which made his dick twitch with anticipation. With the way the man he hoped to soon make his lover pressed against him, he relished the feel of the shifter's hard erection against his own, sending his senses soaring with anticipation.

A wolf whistle rent the air.

Reminded of where he was and what he was supposed to be doing, he broke the kiss. Panting harshly, he licked his lips, trying to catch his breath. He peered into Sage's eyes and grinned.

"Wow," Sage whispered, his eyes dilated with lust. "That was—"

"Yeah," Germaine finished when Sage stopped, obviously struggling to finish.

"Well, well. Is this the reason I gotta tell our boss that you haven't delivered the visitor to him, yet?"

Germaine turned his head and frowned as he stared at a broadly grinning Dakota Drudeson, a fellow enforcer. Rolling his eyes, he ignored the komodo dragon shifter in favor of returning his attention to his mate. While he enjoyed the pinkish hue of Sage's cheeks, he didn't like the embarrassed discomfort flooding his scent.

Cradling Sage's jaw, Germaine teased his thumb under his mate's chin, urging him to lift his head and meet his gaze. "Hey," he crooned. "No need to be upset. It's just Dakota." He cut a smirk the other enforcer's way before fixing his gaze on Sage again. "He has a big mouth on him. Feel free to ignore his lame jokes."

"A-Are you going to get in trouble?" Sage mumbled, his tone full of uncertainty.

Shrugging, Germaine admitted, "I might get a chiding from Mycroft for making him wait, but that'll be all."

Sage's gorgeous green eyes widened. "No, not that." His brows furrowed. "Um, I mean, sorry. That would suck, but—"

Germaine cocked his head as he teased his thumb along Sage's jaw once more. Enjoying the light rasp of Sage's stubble underneath his fingers, he did it again. Feeling his mate press into his touch was even better, and Germaine wondered if the shifter even realized he did it.

"What is it you mean?" Germaine murmured. Out of the corner of his eye, he noticed Dakota speaking into his phone, but the man had moved far enough away that his conversation wasn't disturbing them, which he appreciated. "You can tell me anything."

After a few seconds, where Sage licked his lower lip provocatively, he whispered, "I mean, I'm a man. Are you going to get into trouble for, um, claiming, uh"—he paused and cleared his throat before finishing on a whisper—"that we're m-mates?"

That seemed to yank Dakota away from whoever he was conversing with, probably their boss.

"What did he just say?" Dakota demanded, his expression full of surprise. Still, a smile toyed around the corners of his lips. Before Germaine could even respond, Dakota was at their side, touching his shoulder, and his lips had split into a wide grin. "Tell me I heard what I thought I just heard."

Germaine grinned broadly right back. "You heard that right." Moving his hand from Sage's jaw to his waist, he tucked the shorter male against his side. "This is Sage Kanston, my mate."

Barking a laugh, Dakota slapped Germaine on the upper arm. "Congratulations, you son of a bitch." He shook his head as his expression turned mock angry, although his eyes twinkled, giving him away. "You lucky fucker. I was sure *I* was going to be the next to find a mate."

Shrugging the shoulder of his free arm, Germaine replied smugly, "Well, just goes to show how wrong you can be sometimes." He squeezed Sage's hip before urging him to start moving forward. "Come on, my mate. I'll escort you to Mycroft, and you can tell us why you decided to come and talk about your brother and his crimes."

"Oh, fuck me," Dakota muttered, falling into step beside them. "Kanston. You're Glade Kanston's brother?" Curling his lips, he grumbled, "I'm so sorry, man. Hope you aren't fond of the asshole because he's not gonna return to your pride for a while."

"Uhhhh, what he did was that bad?"

To Germaine's interest, he only heard curiosity in Sage's voice. It was completely devoid of concern. That alone, plus the fact that Sage admitted he was gay, told him just about all he needed to know about the strength of their brotherly relationship.

So why did he come to check on him?

"Afraid so," Dakota replied, opening the door with his key card. "He escorted a rogue into the cafeteria and kitchen. An asshole bent on kidnapping my brother's mate." A low growl entered Dakota's voice, expressing his displeasure.

Germaine couldn't help but point out, "Glade didn't know the shifter was a rogue at the time."

While an asshole, the ex-enforcer had served the council faithfully for decades. He'd just taken the opinion of a councilman as gold, even though it had been proven time and time again that it wasn't true. Councilman Georgio Peregrine was a bigot, just like Glade—*birds of a feather and all that*—and he still held the belief that Fate didn't pair those of the same sex, no matter how many times she proved it otherwise.

Kinda like those weird people who are still claiming the earth is flat even though it's been proven untrue.

Some people just can't be reasoned with.

Dakota's growl brought Germaine back to their conversation. "He was ordered to stand down by Mycroft, and he refused." His green eyes glittered with a hint of malicious amusement as he stated, "Instead, he attacked Delanrue, and my brother had no trouble wiping the floor with his ass."

Sage's eyebrows furrowed as he muttered, "He'd always had a bit of a bully personality, but I'd never heard of him refusing a direct order before." He appeared more confused than anything else. "Did he say why he did that?"

"I wasn't there for his interrogation," Germaine admitted. Pointing a finger at Dakota, he quickly added, "And neither was he. You'll either need to ask Glade or see if Head Enforcer Mycroft will tell you."

As Dakota led the way down one hallway and up another, he commented, "You don't seem overly upset by your brother's incarceration." He eyed Sage speculatively. "Not a close relationship?"

Sage winced, and the scent of guilt perfumed the air. "Uh, well . . ."

"You don't have to answer my nosey friend," Germaine cut in, even though he really wanted to hear the answer to that, too. "Besides, we're here."

With a grateful-looking small smile, Sage nodded. Then he tried to pull away from Germaine as Dakota knocked on the door. Germaine took his turn to growl as he focused on Sage, tightening his hold around his waist.

"What are you doing?" Germaine asked softly even as Mycroft's order to enter reached his ears.

"Um, well," Sage began, glancing nervously toward the

door Dakota was opening. "We're about to see your boss, so —
" He waved between them with his free hand. "Should we
really be going in like this?"

"Yes, we most definitely should," Germaine stated firmly.
Using his thumb, he rubbed over Sage's side as he urged him
forward. "Come on, my mate. Let's get this meeting with my
boss started." With a wink, Germaine added as he guided him
into the spacious office, "After all, the sooner it begins, the
sooner it will end, and we'll be able to go somewhere to get to
know each other better."

"So, Dakota's outburst over the phone is true, Germaine?"
Head Enforcer Mycroft Portent stood next to his desk with his
right hip resting against the huge oak monstrosity. "And this
is Sage Kanston, Glade's brother?"

"Yes, on both counts, Head Enforcer Mycroft," Germaine
replied with a dip of his head. Then he cast a smile Sage's way.
"This is Sage Kanston, and Fate has blessed us. We are mates."

Germaine couldn't keep the pride out of his voice. Even
though he knew nothing about the man pressed against his
side, he didn't care. He believed what he'd said with all his
heart. Fate had blessed him, and he couldn't wait to learn everything about his mate.

Mycroft nodded once, a smile teasing the corners of the
normally serious shifter's lips. "Congratulations to you both,"
he told them. "Finding one's mate is a true gift." Then his gaze
turned serious as he focused on Sage. "Can't pick your family,
huh?"

Sage opened his mouth, then closed it again. A second
later, he murmured, "No. No, you can't." Sounding more confused than ever, he asked, "You just congratulated us. Y-You
don't have a problem that we're both guys?"

With his brows lifting just a smidge, Mycroft asked, "Of
course not. Why would I have a problem with that?"

"W-Well, until I came here, I was under the impression that

Fate didn't couple those of the same sex," Sage replied slowly, obviously being careful to choose his words. His expression tightened a little as he admitted, "And I can't imagine my father being happy about this news." Tipping his head back to meet Germaine's gaze fully, Sage mumbled, "I think I'm going to be kicked out of my pride and named rogue."

Germaine growled softly as he shook his head. "You can't be named rogue for accepting your mate."

"Gods, another pride like that?" Mycroft grumbled, pushing away from his desk. "Grab us drinks, Dakota. Whiskey for me." He moved toward the other half of the office space set up as a fair-sized sitting area with comfortable seating, end tables, and a coffee table—not to mention the sideboard that held a mini-fridge and a couple of decanters on top. "Let's all get comfortable. We have a few things to discuss."

As Germaine guided a clearly confused and uncertain Sage to one of the small, leather sofas, Dakota did as he was told.

All the while, Dakota snarked, "Yeah. Like what asshole is still sharing briefs that say Fate doesn't match those of the same sex."

Germaine wanted to know the same damn thing.

CHAPTER THREE

Sage's mind reeled. His thoughts spun wildly through his brain. As he tried to process everything that was happening to him, he couldn't even tell what drink Germaine had requested for him. After all, Sage had been too busy staring vacantly to formulate an answer.

"Take a sip, Sage," Germaine encouraged, urging the drink he'd pressed into his hand to his lips. "Mycroft is a bit of a whiskey snob, so it's good. Promise."

Acting on instinct, Sage obeyed. He sipped carefully at the drink. While he'd never been one for strong spirits, as the liquid smoothed over his taste buds, he had to admit it was pretty good.

After Sage took a second, then third sip, he finally found his voice. "A-Are there a lot of couples of the same sex paired by Fate?"

"Definitely," Germaine replied, rubbing Sage's neck in a soothing manner. "Whole packs and prides and groups of them."

"Let's change the subject for just a few minutes, Sage," Mycroft told him. "It'll give your brain a few minutes to process while we talk about your brother."

Sage appreciated the idea, and he nodded slowly. "Okay. Thank you, Enforcer Mycroft."

Relaxing back in the cushioned leather chair, Mycroft settled in his seat. "Let's drop the titles while in the confines of my office with just these two, Sage," he ordered, tapping his forefinger against the glass of his tumbler. With a smirk curving his lips, he told him, "While titles have their place, and they are important while interacting within these halls, there's three enforcers in here, so it could end up a little tedious."

Nodding again, Sage murmured, "Yes, sir."

Slinging his arm around Sage's shoulders, Germaine asked, "Why did you come to ask about your brother if you're not close?"

Sage grimaced, uncertain if this subject was much better. Knowing he had to get explanations out of the way, "My father is the head enforcer for my pride."

"You're a lion, too, then?" Germaine cut in curiously.

Realizing it wasn't the first time Germaine had asked, Sage shook his head. "No. I'm a Bengal tiger like my mother. Glade took after my father. They're both lions." He felt his cheeks heat a little since he figured he was giving them information they already had to know. "Um, anyway, my alpha isn't tech-savvy, and he avoids it whenever he can, so my father took over handling emails and electronic reports and stuff."

"Not Beta Larry?" Mycroft asked, revealing he was familiar with who headed up Sage's pride.

Sage couldn't help but snort. "Um, no. Beta Larry is just as bad with tech as Alpha Colton."

"Good to know," Dakota cut in. "It'll make it easy to confirm who's controlling the trickling down of information."

Nodding once more, Sage revealed, "My father doesn't want to leave the area and possibly lose that control, but that's not the only reason I was sent instead of him coming himself."

Germaine grunted. "So you were ordered to come by your father."

"Right."

"Why?" Mycroft pressed. "If he's the one reading the reports, then he would have already known Glade is being charged with the crime of aiding and abetting a rogue, refusing a direct order from his superior, attempted kidnapping of a fated mate, and attacking a fellow council enforcer." Narrowing his eyes, he tipped his chin as a speculative look crossed his features. "Enforcer Bill would also have seen that attacks on fated mates carry harsh punishments, even when there are mitigating circumstances such as in the case of your brother's."

"Mitigating circumstances?" Sage murmured. "What circumstances?"

Dakota curled his lip, expressing his distaste clearly. "Glade worked for Councilman Georgio Peregrine," he told him. "He claims the councilman gave him authorization to escort Shaun, that's the rogue, through the complex."

Confusion flooding Sage anew, he commented, "Councilman Peregrine's name is the one always on the bottom of the reports sent to us. I've seen a few over the years when my father has asked for computer help." Sage lifted his tumbler to his lips, thinking quickly, although nothing was making sense to him. Before taking a sip, he muttered, "Why would a councilman help a rogue?"

"We've been trying to figure out why some ex-councilmen have been helping those willing to hurt shifters for decades," Dakota commented dryly, a sneer darkening his features. "All we can come up with is for the standard reasons—selfishness, bigotry, and greed."

Sage had seen enough of that in his own pride, so he didn't comment on it. Instead, he asked, "So, what did Councilman Peregrine say?" While Sage didn't think he really had the authority to ask for such answers, family loyalty—to his mom, mostly—had him adding, "I mean, if he was following orders, then he shouldn't be in so much trouble, right?"

"Hence the mitigating circumstances," Germaine stated, still teasing his fingertips along Sage's neck.

The movement caused the hairs on Sage's neck and shoulders to stand on end, and his body remained warm and a little on edge.

"The councilman was questioned, and he said he hadn't yet read the report about the troubles in Miggs's pack," Mycroft told Sage, obviously deciding to answer. "He's being asked to pay restitution to Enforcer Delanrue and Miggs, but Glade is the one still in deep water, since he refused my direct order, then went and attacked Delanrue."

Sage rubbed his palm over his dress slacks absently while wondering out loud, "Why would my father send me, then?" Scowling at the floor, Sage murmured, "It was a wasted errand, unless it was just to reassure Glade, which would be typical. He was always Father's favorite."

Germaine squeezed Sage's shoulder lightly, gaining his attention. "How were you supposed to reassure Glade?" The man's dark eyes gleamed with concerned interest as he added, "Words would be of little use. Glade knows the system, and even though he's bitching like crazy, he has to know he was the one in the wrong."

Dakota scoffed with a roll of his eyes. "Yeah, right. Glade take responsibility for his own screw-up?"

From the other enforcer's tone, coupled with his own recollections of his brother's actions, Sage knew it was a rhetorical question. Glade had never owned up to a mistake in his life. It was somehow always someone else's fault.

Instead, Sage reached into his pocket and pulled out a thick signet ring. "Father gave me this to give to him," he revealed. "I was to tell him that his family was always behind him." With a soft snort, Sage told everyone, "Not sure how I was to say it with a straight face, but that was what Dad ordered me to say."

To Sage's surprise, Germaine snatched the ring from his

hand. He held the ring up to the light and squinted at it, turning it this way and that. After a few seconds, Germaine tossed it to Mycroft.

"Hey," Sage cried, frowning at the handsome male. "What are you doing?"

"Sorry, my mate," Germaine soothed, placing his arm back around him and tugging him close again. "This is important." He turned his attention to Mycroft, who was examining the ring. "Is that what I think it is?"

Mycroft growled softly as he nodded. "Yup."

"What is it?" Dakota asked before Sage could.

As Mycroft handed the ring to Dakota, he focused on Sage. "I'm assuming that's your father's ring?" After Sage had nodded, he asked, "Does he wear it often?"

"Almost always," Sage told him. "I was surprised he took it off and handed it to me." Hearing Dakota make a noise of surprise as he stared at the ring, Sage couldn't help but demand, "Why? What's going on?"

Germaine set down his tumbler and rested that hand on Sage's thigh. "I'm sorry, my mate, but your father was setting you up."

Frowning, Sage shook his head. "For what?"

"That ring contains a hidden compartment holding a tiny micro-laser," Mycroft revealed with concern filling his voice. "If Glade had that, he could cut his way through the lock and escape his cell."

"And with his knowledge of our facility, camera placement, and security procedures, he'd have had a very high probability of escaping," Dakota stated with a growl, tossing the ring back to Mycroft. "Damn."

"Damn is right," Germaine snarled, tightening his hold on Sage. "Sage would have been blamed, and since he was none-the-wiser, he would have easily been caught."

A thick lump settled in the back of Sage's throat as he listened to the others continue to discuss the ring. He took a sip of his whiskey, hoping to clear it, but it didn't work. How did one reconcile with the knowledge that his own father had been so willing to trade one son for another?

"I've never seen one of those," Dakota stated, rising from his seat. "Where would he even get it?"

Mycroft held up his own empty tumbler, and Dakota took it on his way to the sideboard. "Outside of the military or CIA or some shadow branch of the government, I have no idea."

"What did he expect Glade to do after he escaped?" Germaine mused, still rubbing Sage's thigh. "Glade had a better chance at a future if he took the time to pay off his crimes."

Sage finally drummed up the courage to interrupt. "I can answer that," he whispered.

Germaine slid his left hand up and threaded it through Sage's hair, scraping over his scalp lightly. "Yeah, babe? What do you think?"

While Sage wasn't a fan of how intensely everyone was looking at him, he forced his voice to come out steady, if a bit soft. "Alpha Colton's youngest daughter is twenty-seven, and he dotes on her. It's a public secret that he'll probably pass the pride on to whoever she mates with."

"Let me guess," Dakota cut in dryly. "Your father wants that to be Glade?"

Sage nodded once. "Glade was supposed to come home for an extended visit in a couple of months. I overheard my father tell Glade over the phone that he was working on getting Alpha Colton to accept Glade's suit to court her." With a snort, Sage couldn't help but add, "Of course, Meribeth never would have been interested. The alpha doesn't know it, but she's into chicks, not dudes." As soon as the secret was out of his mouth, Sage felt his cheeks blaze with shame. "Oh, shit. I shouldn't have said that. Please don't tell anyone."

Germaine dipped his head and pecked a kiss to Sage's temple. "Relax, my mate," he rumbled. "Her secret is safe. No one in this room would out Meribeth."

"Once she's ready, we'd support her though," Dakota told him, handing a fresh drink to Mycroft before retaking his seat. Leaning forward, he rested his forearms on his thighs, holding his own drink between his palms. "We'll offer her a support system."

"Why would you do that?" Sage blurted, glancing between the others. "I wouldn't even consider myself friends with her."

"I'm buddies with your mate," Dakota told him with a wide grin as he straightened. He waggled his eyebrows as he pointed at Germaine. "That makes us buddies, too. She's part of your pride, so if she ends up needing help once it comes out that Fate does pair those of the same sex, we'll be there to offer it."

Sage nodded. "Okay."

Mycroft lifted a hand. "While I agree with Dakota, and it wouldn't only be her we need to start offering support to, you didn't really answer my earlier question," he pointed out. "If your brother escaped and is a wanted shifter, it hardly seems prudent for him to head home and try to woo the alpha's daughter."

Grimacing, Sage hunched his shoulders. "Uh, yeah . . . it would."

"Explain," the head enforcer ordered.

"Remember when I said that my father reviews reports first?" Sage didn't wait for a response. "Well, that means he can hide the fact that Glade is wanted by the council. Alpha Colton and Beta Larry never write their own requests to you all, since they'd need to do it electronically these days." Seeing the frowns on all the men's faces, Sage told them, "Glade could hide in plain sight, and no one would be the wiser, since only Dad would know Glade was a wanted shifter."

Mycroft growled under his breath, but it was Dakota who commented, "But *you* would know."

"Well, sure," Sage replied with a shrug. "But I'm in jail, confused and alone. I'll be asking for help from my parents." Even though it hurt to think about it, Sage accepted the truth. "My dad would probably be telling me that he was doing everything he could, but then he wouldn't actually be doing anything at all. He already had the son he wanted."

Germaine's low growl caused the hair on Sage's neck to stand on end for a whole new reason.

"Your father would leave you in jail while helping to hide Glade?" Dakota sounded scandalized as he shook his head in disgust. "Sometimes I'm glad I lost my parents young. I never had the chance to find out they were assholes."

Unable to help himself, Sage snorted. "Um, lucky you?"

Dakota smirked. "Yeah. Lucky me. Del was the best damn dad a guy could ask for."

Deciding that meant his eldest brother had raised him, Sage nodded as he turned to Mycroft. "What happens now?"

Mycroft's grin appeared predatory. "Well, I now have enough shit on your pride to open an investigation on them," he revealed, his chuckle sounding somewhat sinister as he glanced from Germaine to Dakota and back again. "What do you think? You wanna head to Sage's pride with Investigator Ryzer?"

Germaine barked a laugh. "Oh, yeah. That'll be fun." Sage didn't get the joke, and Germaine must have recognized the scent of his confusion, for his mate grinned at him. "Ryzer is a very skilled investigator. He's a mouse shifter and can play just about any role he needs to fulfill his assignment."

"In this case," Mycroft interrupted with a grin. "We'll have him look like a flamboyant twink."

"Oh, that'll piss off the powers that be," Dakota crowed,

laughing.

Mycroft's green eyes twinkled. "I'll get in touch with the councilmen we need in order to get permission to get this investigation started."

"And while they do that" —Germaine rose to his feet and held out his hand—"you and I will spend some time alone and get to know each other better."

Even as nerves filled Sage at what the future could hold flooded his system, he felt equal parts excitement, too.

For better or worse, as Sage took Germaine's hand and allowed him to pull him to his feet, Sage knew his life was about to change.

CHAPTER FOUR

Germaine figured he was steamrolling his mate, but he didn't give a shit. With the idea of Sage being put in harm's way, by his own father no less, his instincts screamed at him to get him somewhere safe. Germaine needed him tucked into his suite, where he could hold him close and get to know him.

And do other things.

Upon hearing the lecherous voice in his head, Germaine fought back a smirk. He definitely wanted to do other things. Things that included more of the kissing they'd done in the parking garage.

Doing his best to ignore his insistent boner, Germaine guided Sage to an elevator. He pushed the down button. While waiting for the carriage, he teased his hand up and down Sage's spine through his jacket.

"I know shifters who meet their mates do things fast," Germaine began slowly, hoping Sage wouldn't ask for time. "But I really want to claim you before we head back to your pride lands."

Hell, I'll tie Sage to my bed and torture him with bliss until he agrees if that's what it takes to convince him.

Germaine felt the tremble work through Sage's body beneath his fingertips. Meeting his gaze, his pretty tiger admitted, "I really want that, too." Sage scoffed softly. "No one ever told me about the insane pull you immediately feel when you meet your mate."

Understanding completely, Germaine stated, "It's intense." The doors opened, and he urged him inside as he added, "I've seen a number of friends go through it over the years. Now that the Shifter Council is cleaning out the riff-raff, Fate has started blessing us with finding our mates."

"What kind of riff-raff?"

Pushing the button to go up two floors, which would take them to the floor housing the enforcer's living quarters, Germaine explained, "The usual. Power-hungry and corrupt leaders. We're not all the way there yet, but we've made great strides in the last few years." He rested both hands on Sage's hips and peered into his mate's warm green eyes. "Except, I don't want to talk about *them*."

Feeling Sage rest his hands on his chest, Germaine's body flushed hot, and his nipples beaded.

"What do you want to talk about?"

Germaine loved the slightly breathy quality of Sage's voice. "You, me, and a bed," he rumbled gruffly. "Please tell me you're a switch because even though I want to fuck and claim you in the worst way, I look forward to feeling you take me, too."

At Germaine's blunt words, he watched Sage's green eyes deepen to a gorgeous jade. The scent of his arousal flooded the confined space. Even his nostrils flared, and his breathing hitched audibly.

"Ohhhh," Germaine crooned, sidling closer. "You do like the sound of that."

"Yes," Sage hissed, sliding his hands up and resting them on Germaine's shoulders.

"I'm very glad he likes it, too, but I doubt we needed to know about it."

The sound of a deep, droll voice jerked Germaine's attention to the left. He saw that the elevator doors had opened without him noticing.

29

Enforcer Dane stood with a hand on the door, holding them open and smirking at him. Behind the enforcer, with a faint smile teasing the edges of his lips, stood Councilman Regales Colearian, a grizzly shifter who'd helped champion many of the changes to the council after finding his own mate in a human male. That human, Theo Conway, stood with them, and he appeared to be barely holding back a laugh.

"Uh, sorry, Councilman," Germaine quickly stated, dipping his head in deference to the other male. He could practically feel the heat of Sage's blush as his mate bowed his head and mumbled the same. In order to help ease his tiger's unease, Germaine focused on Dane and stated, "Don't rain on my parade, man. You're just jealous you haven't found your mate so you can do all the kinky shit you love."

Regales opened his mouth, but Theo beat him to words. "You're into kinky shit, Dane?" The human cocked his head as he stared at him with narrowed eyes. "How come you never mentioned it?"

Dane groaned, his expression turning put upon. "I'm not into kinky shit," he muttered, shaking his head. "Not that my sex life is anyone's business."

"Well, you did start the talk of sex lives," Regales claimed as he wrapped his arm possessively around Theo. "And while I care about you, old friend, I'm not certain I care about you *that* much."

Germaine knew Regales teased. Even though Dane worked almost exclusively as the councilman's private guard, which meant he would put his life on the line for him if necessary, they really were close friends. Before Theo had ended up in Regales's life, Germaine would have bet that Dane was his closest confidant.

"Oh, good grief," Dane grumbled, shaking his head. Pointing his thumb over his shoulder, he focused on Germaine and snapped, "Get out of there, so we can get to our meeting."

Chuckling, Germaine grabbed Sage's hand and tugged him out of the carriage behind him.

The trio immediately filed inside, but Regales placed his hand on the door to keep it open, so Germaine paused.

"Congratulations, Germaine," Regales stated, smiling. He focused on Sage. "You couldn't have landed yourself a better enforcer." Then Regales winked. "Unless you'd been matched up with Dane, of course."

Germaine scowled, but before he could figure out an appropriate come-back, Sage beat him to it. "Thank you, Councilman. I appreciate that." His tone remained steady as he continued, "But I figure Fate knows what she's doing, because it sounds like Dane wouldn't be able to keep up with my kinkiness."

While Dane's cheeks took on a pinkish hue, Theo tipped his head back and laughed. Even the councilman chuckled as he released the door. "Have fun," he called with a wave before disappearing from view.

Tugging Sage after him, Germaine admitted with a smile, "I can't wait to hear all about this kinkiness, my mate."

Sage scoffed. "I'm not really into anything kinky, but I couldn't resist," he told him. "Not like my occasional fuck buddies. Randy loves to watch me fuck Cain while fingering his own ass, getting himself ready for my dick next. He—"

Germaine couldn't stand to hear more. Pressing Sage's back against the nearest door, he slammed his mouth over his mate's. He delved between his lips, plundering and demanding surrender.

Upon feeling Sage's arms around his neck and his body pushing pliantly against his own, Germaine softened the kiss. He wrapped his right arm around the shifter's waist, clutching him close. Threading his fingers into Sage's thick, dirty-blond hair, he tugged his mate's head to the perfect angle.

Then Germaine deepened the kiss once more. He lapped at

Sage's tongue. He nibbled his lips. He mapped his mouth with deep, penetrating strokes in a parody of what he planned to do with his cock.

Finally, when breathing became a need and not a desire, Germaine lifted his head. He panted harshly as he took in Sage's pink cheeks and dilated eyes. The lustful glaze in Sage's green orbs sent Germaine's need into overdrive—his need to stare into that look while fucking him into the mattress.

"You're mine," Germaine ground out as soon as he had enough air in his lungs. "I will never share you."

While Germaine had partaken in a few ménages over the couple of centuries of his life, it had never really been his thing. It sounded as if Sage did it often. Uneasiness filled Germaine that he wouldn't be enough for his mate.

"The idea of sharing you turns my stomach," Sage whispered, rubbing up and down his chest. "Is that normal?" Teasing his fingertips along Germaine's jaw, he softly admitted, "I've never been in a relationship so I don't know."

Germaine let go of his discomfort, mentally reminding himself that Fate wouldn't have paired them if they weren't compatible . . . in every way.

Massaging his mate's scalp, Germaine told Sage, "I've seen a number of mated pairs come together over the last few years, and every time, they become hella-possessive of each other." He released Sage's hair in favor of teasing his fingertips over the tiger shifter's eyebrow, mapping his features. "Even hearing you talk about fucking another—" Germaine snapped his mouth shut, but a growl still rumbled up his throat.

"Hey," Sage murmured, rubbing his hands over Germaine's shaved scalp. "I didn't mean to upset you. It didn't even occur to me how my words could be taken." His expression turned earnest as he continued, "With the way my tiger is calling for me to mark you, so all the world will know you're mine, something I very much want, too, even though logically, I know there are so many things we should discuss first, I can't imagine allowing another to touch you, so of course it makes sense that you'd feel the same. I—"

"Hush," Germaine scolded softly, pecking Sage's lips once more. He could think of no better way to silence his soon-to-be lover's babbling. "Let's get in my suite, so we can purge some of these raging hormones." Never would Germaine have realized that finding his mate would make him randier than a teenager. "After we're done fucking each other's brains out, we'll lie naked in bed and talk about all that other shit."

Sage groaned, his eyelids sliding to half-mast. "Yes, please."

Beyond delighted that his mate agreed, Germaine eased his body away from Sage's. He spotted his door four feet down the hall. Grabbing Sage's hand, he damn near dragged his mate to it, unwilling to allow him to get that far away from him.

To Germaine's relief, Sage came willingly, even going so far as to tuck his other hand into the waistband of his pants. He unlocked his door, unable to fight the shiver that worked down his spine upon feeling his mate's fingers slide over his flesh so near his ass-crack. His chute clenched as anticipation churned in his gut.

Fast or not, Germaine wasn't going to wait an instant longer.

Germaine ensconced them both in his suite, closing and locking the door behind him. Without preamble, he tugged his shirt over his head while leading the way through the front lounging area. As he crossed the threshold into his bedroom, he tossed his work polo in the direction of his closet.

That was when Germaine felt Sage tug on a belt loop. Turning, he spotted the way his mate nibbled his bottom lip. His uncertainty nearly tore a hole in Germaine's gut.

Did I misunderstand?

"What is it, my mate?" Germaine asked, taking both of Sage's hands in his own. "What's wrong?"

"Wrong?" Sage's brows shot up. "Nothing's wrong." Understanding seemed to dawn across his features, for he lost his nervous expression and smiled. "Sorry. I just. Well. I've been driving for the last almost twelve hours except for fuel, food, and restroom breaks." Tugging his right hand free, Sage pointed through an open doorway that obviously led into a bathroom. "Do you mind if I clean up? It'd really make me more comfortable before we" —he cleared his throat— "you know."

"Oh, we'll definitely" —Germaine waggled his eyebrows as he released Sage's other hand— "*you know*." Taking a step backward, he filled his voice with innuendo as he told him, "I'll just be in here getting comfortable."

Sage must have caught his drift, for his cheeks darkened. His Adam's apple bobbed at his throat as he swallowed. Even as Sage took a step toward the bathroom, his focus slid over Germaine's naked torso as if he couldn't tear his gaze away.

Germaine loved that response, but he wanted his mate naked and comfortable even more. "Get cleaned up, Sage," he ordered, moving toward the bed. "Don't keep me waiting too long, please, my mate."

His head bobbing in a nod, Sage turned away and hurried into the bathroom.

Sitting on the bed, Germaine quickly untied and removed his boots. He tugged his socks off as he rose back to his feet. After grabbing his shirt from the floor, he entered his closet. In seconds, Germaine was naked, and his clothes were in the dirty clothes basket.

Returning to the bedroom, Germaine eyed the bed. His throbbing cock led the way as he made his way to it. He was so very tempted to take himself in hand and give himself some stimulation, but he resisted . . . barely.

For now.

Germaine yanked the comforter to the foot of the bed. Pulling open the nightstand, he picked up his bottle of lube. After closing the drawer, Germaine climbed onto the bed and adjusted the pillows so he could sit with his lower back against the headboard.

With his legs spread a little, giving his heavy balls more room, Germaine got himself as comfortable as possible while waiting for his mate and anticipating the best sex of his life. As he squirted a dollop of lube onto the palm of his right hand, he figured this wasn't the most romantic way for their first time. Mentally, he vowed to make it up to Sage.

Germaine just needed his mate too damn badly.

As Germaine took his erection in hand, he heard the water run in the bathroom. He sighed as he gave himself a bit of light friction, all the while wondering what his mate was up to. Had Sage stripped, too, or was he still clothed? Were the nest of curls around Sage's cock the same shade as the dirty-blond waves on his head, or were they darker? Germaine wondered how pink his soon-to-be lover's erection would become in his time of need and couldn't wait to find out.

When his balls began to tighten, Germaine stopped stroking. He pinched the base of his erection, sending a shock of pain through him. With his other hand, he gripped his balls and tugged.

Germaine sighed as his impending release eased.

The click of the bathroom's doorknob caught Germaine's attention. He didn't know when the sound of running water had disappeared. His thoughts of his sexy mate had distracted him fully.

As the door swung open, revealing Sage, Germaine felt his need for release roar through his veins anew. For an instant, his mate stared pensively at him. Germaine's expression — or his naked reclined form—seemed to bolster his shifter's confidence.

Sage sauntered toward him in all his naked glory. His lightly bronzed skin over taut muscle glowed in the overhead light. His pubic curls were cropped short, a darker hue than what was on his head. Sage's erection jutted long and proud from within them, a thick length of maybe eight glorious inches that Germaine couldn't wait to bathe with his tongue.

"Oh, gods, Gere," Sage muttered, stopping at the edge of the bed. "The way you're looking at me. Gonna make me blow without a touch."

Yanking his focus to Sage's face, Germaine spotted the blatant need etched over his features. "Well," he drawled as his mouth watered. "Let's not let it go to waste, then."

Before Sage could respond, Germaine rolled to his knees, leaned over, and swallowed Sage's erection to the root.

Germaine heard Sage's cry of pleasure—the noise almost drowned out by his own moan of delight as his mate's earthy, masculine flavor burst across his taste buds.

Delicious.

CHAPTER FIVE

"Gere!" Sage cried, instinctively gripping his mate's bald head for some kind of support. "Oh, fuck. Gere!"

Sage tried to ease back, to get away from the spine-tingling pressure building in his gut. Except, Germaine wouldn't allow it. His mate had latched one dark hand onto his ass, and he refused to allow him to withdraw too far before tugging him in deep again.

With the way his balls were tightening beyond any hope of control, Sage knew he was going to come embarrassingly fast. He couldn't help it. The snake shifter's blowjob talents were a thing of decadence.

Germaine would draw halfway off his cock, sucking hard while teasing over his flared head. He would pause there for a heartbeat, tapping the tip of his tongue against his frenulum, sending tingles straight to Sage's balls. Then Germaine would take him in deep again, somehow managing to lick over damn near every sensitive bit of his length.

With a cry of ecstasy, Sage lost control. His hips bucked, sinking him deep into Germaine's hot mouth. His erection throbbed while his testicles drew up, and his cum pulsed up his shaft.

Without missing a beat, Germaine swallowed around him, drinking every burst Sage provided. His thighs trembled as waves of zinging bliss rocked through his system. The skin of his groin goose bumped, and he shuddered, barely staying upright.

When Sage finally came back to himself, he discovered

he'd half draped over Germaine's head. His mate still held the crown of his penis between his lips. He suckled ever-so-lightly, keeping him stimulated and hard.

Or that could be the finger in my ass.

Sage finally registered the light massage to his prostate. Moaning, his gut clenching, he tried to straighten. His knees trembled, making it difficult, but he managed it.

Germaine eased up on his knees, releasing his prick. At the same time, he pulled his finger from Sage's channel.

Immediately missing the sensation, Sage hissed.

"Come up here, Sage," Germaine urged, gripping his upper arm with his clean hand. He placed his slightly sticky fingers on Sage's hip. "Lie down, my mate. Take a load off." The big black man grinned lasciviously as he helped him onto the bed. "And let me have my wicked way with you."

Sage chuckled huskily as he obeyed Germaine's urgings. After flopping onto his back, he grinned up at the larger man levering over him. He lifted his hands and rubbed up and down his forearms.

"I'm pretty sure you already did that," Sage teased, enjoying the feel of the ropy muscle underneath his fingers.

Germaine eased between Sage's knees as he placed his palms on his ribcage. "Oh, I have so many more plans for you, Sage." As Germaine skimmed his fingers down Sage's torso, his expression sobered a smidge. "I know this isn't romantic or even very sensual, but I will make it up to you. I hope to have centuries to learn every inch of your body . . . over and over again."

Squeezing Germaine's arms, Sage assured, "I don't care about sensual or romantic. All I care about is that we please each other in and out of bed." He rubbed his hands over his lover's smooth, dark flesh. "So far, I think we're off to a good start on both counts."

Even as Germaine began to nod, his eyebrows were still furrowed.

Sage decided that wouldn't do at all. Peering right, then left, he spotted what he wanted. He grabbed the tube of lube Germaine must have used at some point, considering the slick digit which had been in his ass.

Something I want more of . . . now, dammit.

Germaine held out his hand, so Sage dutifully added more to the man's fingers instead of giving him the tube. His mate didn't question him, but his black brows did shoot up when Sage poured a little onto his own fingers. Then Sage closed the tube with a flick of his thumb and tossed it back to the mattress.

"What are you—" Germaine hissed, not finishing his sentence.

Sage had answered his lover before he could even finish the thought . . . by wrapping his fingers around Germaine's jutting cock and jacking it slowly. The strong frame hovering over him shuddered, which sent a wealth of smug satisfaction through Sage. He played with Germaine's dick, learning his length and girth by feel as he admired the lines of pleasure-pain passing over his new and forever lover's face in waves.

Germaine gritted his teeth ferally, a shudder working over him. His cock twitched in Sage's grip. When a bead of pre-cum oozed from the slit that gaped with every downstroke of his hand, Sage licked his lips, his mouth watering in anticipation.

"Sage, fuck!" Germaine whined. "Gods, you gotta stop, or I'm gonna blow all over you." With dilated eyes, he levered back, pulling away from Sage's hold. He pinned him with a hungry look as he raked his gaze over him. "And as much as I want to smear my cum all over your skin, we'll have to do that another time."

Groaning at that imagery, Sage lifted his arms. "Yes, please." He waggled his fingers, hoping Germaine would draw close again. "Another time. I need you in my ass too bad to wait. Come here."

Germaine groaned even as he nodded and drew close to him again. "Gotta finish stretching you," he panted, sweat beading on his upper lip, betraying his strain. "Won't hurt you."

"I won't need much prep," Sage countered, spreading his legs wider in invitation. "I love the burn and can't wait to feel your long spear delving deep into my body."

To Sage's pleasure, another visible shudder worked through his mate. His eyes were so widely dilated that he wondered how the other man could focus. How his mate reacted to him sent his own pleasure skyrocketing, his body nearly vibrating with need even though he'd come just a few minutes before.

"Sage," Germaine rumbled even as he eased one long slender finger deep into Sage's channel. "Gonna fill you up so good. Gonna reach so far up your ass." As Germaine spoke, he eased his digit out before pressing two into him. "Can't wait to feel you wrapped around me."

Willing his body to relax, Sage murmured, "Yeah. Now. Need you now." He knew what his body could take and couldn't wait to feel the nearly foot-long piece of meat Germaine sported. While Sage had never considered himself a size queen, his body screamed to feel his mate's jutting cock buried deep inside him. Gripping Germaine's wrist, Sage tugged at it as he rocked his hips. "Get your dick in me, goddamnit!"

To Sage's relief, Germaine pulled his fingers free. Then, to his annoyance, he grabbed both of his wrists and forced them over his head. His long dick tapped against Sage's own as he met his gaze with a feral grin.

"So eager, Sage," Germaine growled with a feral smile. His dark eyes glimmered in the light, appearing almost black with his desire. "Gonna make you mine for all time."

"Yes, please," Sage whispered. "Now."

As Sage held Germaine's gaze, seeing his lover peer at him intently, he wondered what the other man was looking for. He almost opened his mouth to ask. Resisting took every bit of self-control he possessed.

Finally, when Sage was about to give in to the urge—or maybe flip him over and ride his cock like a pogo stick—Germaine ordered, "Lift your legs and wrap them around my waist."

Sage immediately obeyed, slinging them around Germaine's lean hips. Peering between them, he watched impatiently as his lover adjusted his hips and lined up his cock with his hole. At the first press of his mate's flared crown, Sage pushed out, welcoming his forever mate into his body.

When Germaine's dick popped into him, Sage bit back his hiss, uncertain how his lover would take the noise. He felt his dick flex at the pleasing burn of the stretch. His mate had seemed so concerned, and he didn't want him to stop.

We'll learn each other in time.

"You okay?" Germaine rasped.

Snapping open eyelids Sage didn't remember closing, he met Germaine's concerned gaze. He clenched and released around his mate's prick, enjoying the delicious stretch. Sage enjoyed the way Germaine's eyes nearly rolled to the back of his head while his mate's low throaty groan was even better.

"Sage?"

Relishing the sound of his name in Germaine's throaty, needy whine, Sage tightened his legs and rocked his hips. "I'm so good, Gere," he assured, doing his best to encourage his mate. "Would be better if you sank your gorgeous erection in the rest of the way."

To Sage's surprise, Germaine grinned broadly at him. "Do you always top from the bottom?"

Sage gaped for an instant, then barked a laugh. "Uh, maybe?"

Germaine chuckled as he lowered until his chest rested against Sage's own. "Guess I better give you what you want then," he purred as he slid his right hand under Sage's left thigh to grip his ass cheek. With his dark eyes gleaming with desire, Germaine ordered, "Hang on tight, my mate."

Before Sage could figure out what Germaine was talking about, he slid his second hand under his back and gripped his shoulder from behind. Then Germaine slammed his hips forward.

Sage groaned with delight as Germaine's long slender rod sank deep into his body. Arching his back and tightening his legs, he did his best to keep that pleasant stretching tool as deeply inside him as he could. Except, the second Germaine's pubes tickled his ass cheeks, his mate began pulling out again.

Before Sage could issue a complaint, Germaine covered him from shoulders to torso. "I got you, my mate," he crooned into his ear as he pushed back into his body. "I'll never leave you hanging."

Then Germaine pulled out and pushed in again . . . and again . . . and again.

"That's the way, baby," Germaine crooned into his ear, adjusting his angle. "That's the way you want it, isn't it?"

Pleasure spiked through Sage's rectum as his mate nailed his prostate over and over. "Yesssss," he hissed, rocking into each of Germaine's jolting thrusts. His body felt on fire as heat spread through his groin and out his limbs. "Gere, yes!"

Germaine growled in his ear, the sound low and intense. "Yeah, that's the way." Somehow, he managed to speed up his thrusts while continuing to hit his pleasure button. "Shout my name, Sage. Show me you know it's me fucking you through the mattress, claiming your ass as my own."

Sage's breathing stuttered in his chest. His cock throbbed between them. Digging his fingernails into Germaine's back, he arched his neck, fighting his urge to come.

"Shout for me, Sage," Germaine urged, snapping his hips hard against him, driving him into the mattress. "Now, baby. Gonna fucking fill your ass."

Between hearing Germaine's encouragement, the hard jolts to Sage's prostate, and his lover's tight hold as he pressed him into the mattress, Sage could do little else. He moaned his mate's name over and over as he rocked into his mate. His thighs trembled as his cock throbbed, even as his balls pulled tight.

"Gere, please," Sage whined, a new need surfacing within him. He tipped his head to the side. "Claim me."

"I will, Sage," Germaine snarled gruffly. "Coat me with your seed first. I wanna feel it."

Groaning, Sage shuddered upon hearing Germaine's demand. He whimpered as he felt his erection slide over his mate's sweat-slicked abdominals. His cock leaked against the flesh as his balls began to pull tighter and tighter with each pound to his prostate.

"That's it," Germaine encouraged, obviously feeling some changes in his body. "So good." He pulled his left hand from beneath his shoulder, pushing him even harder into the mattress, so he could reach between them. "Now . . . come."

Then Germaine wrapped his fingers around Sage's cock tightly and jacked him. Two was all it took before Sage's dick erupted. His orgasm flooded him with wave after wave of blissful endorphins.

"Gere!"

Sage cried his mate's name before he lost his voice to a moan. He clung to Germaine, feeling his lover slam into his hole one last time before heat filled him from the inside out. His mind floated with the knowledge that he'd pleased his lover.

Feeling Germaine's teeth at his neck, Sage tilted his head even more. "Yes," he slurred.

"Yessss," Germaine hissed. "Mine."

In the next instant, Germaine's teeth pierced Sage's flesh. The spike of pain almost immediately morphed into the headiest surge of tingles. They flushed his body with heat, settling in his balls.

Another orgasm blindsided Sage, sending him tumbling over the edge as each suck of Germaine's mouth to his neck pulsed more bliss through him.

Sage drifted pleasantly for several heartbeats until he felt Germaine ease his teeth free and lick over the wound. Then his animal demanded him to return the bite. Happy to give in to his instincts, Sage lifted his head, wrapped his jaw around Germaine's flesh, and sank in his teeth.

The succulent flavor of Germaine's life-giving fluid flowed across his tongue, causing his senses to sing. He hummed with pleasure and sucked for more. Hearing Germaine's groan, feeling his lover's fingers dig into his flesh where he held him, and feeling the sensation of heat fill his rectum anew, Sage knew he'd caused his mate to come.

Easing his teeth free, Sage licked his lips and swallowed. Then he slid his tongue over the wound, lapping up the last few drops and sealing it. He stared at his mating mark, satisfaction causing his animal to purr in the back of his mind.

"Gods, Sage," Germaine mumbled, nuzzling Sage's neck. "That was so fucking good." Lifting his head, he met his gaze and gave him a lascivious smile. "I can't wait to do it again, but with your cock in my ass."

Sage chuckled as his prick gave a little twitch. "I'm sure we can make that happen," he replied, even though he figured it would be some time before he could actually get it up again.

"I look forward—"

The trill of Sage's cell phone reached his ears, and he groaned—this time, not in a good way.

"I'm sorry," Sage mumbled, frustration flooding him as he

pushed at Germaine's shoulder. "That's my father's ring tone. I should really get it."

Germaine nodded, easing off of him and the bed. "Okay. I'll grab a cloth to clean us up while you do."

Grateful his mate wasn't upset, Sage took his tall, strong shifter's hand and followed him into the bathroom.

CHAPTER SIX

As Sage answered his phone, Germaine grabbed a clean hand towel and ran it under warm water. He wiped himself down while watching his mate move back into the bedroom, most likely to escape the weird bathroom echo that always seemed to happen in the space. Germaine listened unabashedly, since Sage had only moved away a few steps.

"Hello, Father."

"Have you seen Glade, yet?" a deep voice demanded without out a greeting.

Germaine rubbed the cloth over his belly, cock, and balls as he narrowed his eyes in displeasure upon hearing the way Bill spoke to his mate.

"No, Father. Not yet. I—"

"Why the hell not?" Bill cut in. "Your appointment with Mycroft was an hour and a half ago. That's plenty of time."

Sage glanced Germaine's way, an uncertain look on his face.

Wishing to offer Sage some encouragement, Germaine smiled reassuringly as he winked. Then he turned the water back on and began rinsing the cloth.

"Well, for some reason, I think they were expecting you or Mom," Sage said into the phone. "And because I'm just his brother, they're making me wait."

Germaine turned the water back off and wrung it out before heading into the bedroom. While he scented the slight acrid smell that told him Sage was blatantly lying to his father, he knew the man wouldn't be able to tell through the phone.

Smirking, Germaine lowered to one knee before his mate, resting one hand on his hip.

"Damn those stupid bureaucratic fuckers," Bill roared into the phone, which probably ended up a good thing, since his words drowned out Sage's soft *eep* as Germaine began wiping down his groin. Sage stared at him with wide eyes, hardly paying attention to his father as the man continued, "Then what the hell have you been doing? You should be sitting on them and pestering them to see Glade. You need to give him my ring."

Germaine frowned upon hearing his continued demands. Dipping his head a little, he turned his focus to cleaning his mate as he listened to Sage reply. His mate stumbled over his words a little, and Germaine figured he wasn't helping his lover concentrate, since he picked up one of Sage's feet and placed it on his upturned thigh, allowing him to reach Sage's lube and cum-covered hole and inner thighs.

"I, uh, um, I-I'm in a suite a-at headquarters," Sage stuttered. "So, I'm still here. I-I'll try to call H-Head Enforcer Mycroft as soon as I get off the phone with you."

"Good. You do that," Bill demanded. "Let me know as soon as you see Glade." His voice lowered to a cold tone. "And it better be soon, Sage. Don't disappoint me."

"Yes, Father."

While Germaine didn't care for the subservient notes in Sage's tone, he figured it was a conditioned response. He hoped that, when they met the pride enforcer in person, it wouldn't create problems. Germaine hated that he was going to be asking Sage to put his mating before his family, but —

No, wait. That will be what Bill is doing. Family should support and celebrate a fated mating, regardless of who it's with.

Germaine didn't hear their goodbyes and didn't know if it was because they didn't say any or if it was because he'd been too lost in his thoughts.

"So, uh, how exactly did you expect me to concentrate on

47

my father with you doing that?" Sage grumbled, although his scent screamed his amusement, as did his smile.

With a wink, Germaine rose back to his feet. "Well, since I didn't really want you having to concentrate long on that asshole, I figure it worked," he teased. Heading to the open closet door, he tossed the soiled cloth into the basket while saying, "How about we lie back down and do some of that post-coital pillow talk your father's shitty timing made us miss out on?"

"Sounds good to me," Sage replied, sliding his gaze over Germaine's frame with an appreciative gleam in his eyes. "It'll give me time to tease my fingertips over every line of your body."

Growling softly, Germaine followed Sage to the bed. "I do like the sound of that."

Sage placed his phone on the nightstand, then began crawling onto the mattress. "Me, too."

"Hold up," Germaine ordered, noticing the wet spot. "Give me a sec."

Then Germaine hurried back to the bathroom. He grabbed a towel off the rack and returned to the bedroom. Spreading it out, he placed it over the dampness.

With a grin, Germaine stated, "We can strip the sheets later." Then he guided Sage to the middle of the bed. He flopped onto his back and pulled his mate into his arms. "Come here."

To Germaine's pleasure, Sage came easily. His mate rested his head on his shoulder with an arm and leg flopped over him. True to his word, Sage began running his fingertips over the muscular lines of Germaine's torso.

Humming appreciatively, Germaine did a little exploring of his own. He rubbed up and down Sage's back, teasing each knob of his spine. With his other hand, he gripped the ass cheek of the leg he had sprawled over Germaine's thighs, massaging over the perfect handful.

For several long moments, they lay together in silence, just enjoying each other's touch.

Finally, Sage grumbled, "So, uh, I guess I still need to see Glade."

"Only for a moment," Germaine assured. "You can tell your father that we confiscated the ring. Having it would be against prisoner protocol."

While that wasn't strictly true for jewelry in general, because it wasn't a simple ring, it was a factual statement.

Sage nodded against his chest. "Okay." Then he tipped his head up a little and asked, "How old are you?"

Germaine lifted his head and pecked a kiss to Sage's lips before relaxing back again. "I'll be two hundred forty-three as of this spring," he told his mate. "But my driver's license says thirty-eight. What about you?"

As a shifter who lived upward of five hundred years, they had to remake their identities every few decades.

"One hundred twenty-three," Sage replied. "And my license says I'm thirty-one."

Chuckling, Germaine winked and said, "You don't look a day over eighty-seven."

Pleasure filled him when Sage chuckled and rolled his eyes. In truth, his mate barely appeared thirty. Shifters stopped aging in their prime, remaining looking the same for most of their lives. That was the reason they had to fake their deaths and change their identities regularly, since the invention of electronics meant they couldn't just move somewhere new.

"How long have you been a council enforcer?" Sage asked, skimming a fingertip along one groove of his abdominals. "Have you always wanted to be one?"

"I sort of fell into it," Germaine told Sage, thinking about his past—oh, so long ago. "It's a bit of a long story," he warned. "You sure you want to hear it?"

Sage immediately nodded. "You're my mate. I want to know everything about you."

Warmth flooding his chest that had nothing to do with arousal, Germaine smiled at Sage as he pressed a light kiss to his lips. "Snakes don't live in tight-knit groups like many shifters, but we were part of a coalition of about two dozen anaconda shifters," he began, thinking of things he hadn't in a long, long time. "Two hundred years ago, we lived in the Amazon, but slash and burn farming drove us out."

"Damn, I'm sorry."

Germaine shrugged the shoulder Sage wasn't leaning on. "It was a long time ago. Anyway, we traveled to the Florida Keys with a few other shifters. My father picked up work as a dock worker, and my mother cleaned the homes of the wealthy." Smiling at his memories, Germaine recalled, "I remember Father always coming home exhausted, but they were happy." His smile slipped from his lips as he finished, "One day, a fire broke out on the docks, and he died saving several other workers, including another anaconda shifter. My parents were fated mates, so my mother passed soon after. None of the other shifters wanted to care for a twelve-year-old boy, so they contacted the Shifter Council, and I was sent to them."

Sage gaped at him. "Even the dock worker your father saved refused to take you in?"

Shaking his head, Germaine admitted, "I ran across him decades later, and he apologized. He was young at the time and wouldn't have been able to properly care for me anyway." He teased his fingertips over Sage's neck, enjoying the contact. "I remember it being scary at the time. I was twelve. Confused, lonely, scared, and sad."

"What happened?" Sage asked, peering at him with anticipation. "Did you get placed with someone nice?"

Germaine chuckled as he thought of Cruz Blodwen. Nice

was not a word anyone would ever use to describe him. "Not nice, no," he admitted. "But he was a good man. My guardian was Councilman Cruz Blodwen, an anaconda shifter sitting on the council at the time. I'd call him firm but understanding." As Germaine thought of his teenage years with Cruz, he couldn't help but smile. "A disappointed look from Cruz worked better than any belt. Making that man proud by becoming a Council Guard, then an enforcer, were some of the best moments of my life." Cradling Sage's jaw, Germaine met his mate's gaze. "Until I met you."

Sage smiled back at him, his green eyes filled with answering warmth. "You talk about him as if he's no longer living," he murmured uncertainly.

"He's not," Germaine confirmed. "He died almost a hundred years ago. He was replaced by Councilman Lorian Bakerman, a buffalo shifter." Upon seeing the platitudes coming a mile away, Germaine touched his fingertips to Sage's lips. "Don't apologize or be sorry. I've moved past the grief and enjoy sharing about Cruz. He was truly a great man."

"Okay," Sage murmured. "I'd love to hear about him sometime, then."

Germaine nodded. "Sounds good, but we're talking about us right now." Sliding his forefingers over his jaw, he admired how his dark skin appeared next to his mate's light-bronze flesh. "What about you? What do you do, and do you enjoy it?"

"My pride lives near a little tourist town north of Boston," Sage revealed. "There's this candy and sweets shop there run by a wonderful, older couple. I work for them."

"A sweets shop, huh?" Germaine grinned broadly. "You're a baker?"

Sage scoffed. "Uh, no," he denied, shaking his head. "Sorry. If you were hoping for a baker, you're totally out of luck." Grimacing, he admitted, "I can burn water. I either eat out, eat out of a box, get food from my mother, or food from Misses Ellen." When Germaine arched his brow in silent question, Sage explained, "She's the wife in the pair who owns the sweet shop. Everyone calls her that. Her husband is Walter Divord."

"What kind of sweets shop, then?" Germaine didn't bother trying to contain his curiosity.

"Sweets of all kinds. Gummies, taffy, toffee, chocolates, and everything in between." With a grin, Sage told him, "They even have those little sugar dot things that come on a strip of paper and you eat them off with your teeth."

"Oh wow." Germaine hummed as his mouth watered. "I love cinnamon bears. When we're there, we'll definitely have to hit it up."

Sage began to nod, but just as quickly, he furrowed his brows. "From that comment, I'm going to guess that you expect me to move here."

Germaine opened his mouth, then snapped it shut again. He grimaced. Finally, he nodded once. "Guess that was pretty big-headed of me, huh?"

Sighing, Sage slid his gaze down and focused on Germaine's nipple as he teased his fingertip around and around it.

While Germaine found it caused wonderful sensations to spark through his chest and trickle down his torso, he moved his hand from Sage's delectable rear end. He wrapped his hand around Sage's, stopping his distracting movement. A squeeze to his mate's fingers pulled the tiger shifter's attention back to him.

"I'm sorry, Sage," Germaine told him. "What are your thoughts on moving here? Do you think it would be something you'd consider?" Not giving Sage time to answer right away, Germaine added, "I could look for a job in your area, but how close is your shop to your pride's lands? Will they cause trouble?"

Sage sighed deeply. The hint of a smile curved his lips although his scent turned a bit sad. "No. You're right," he murmured, shaking his head. "I can imagine my father and inner circle creating trouble for us, and I'd never bring that kind of crap down on Misses Ellen's head." Sage returned Germaine's squeeze on his hand. "I do want to give her my notice in person, but it'll have to be after I've told Alpha Colton, Beta Larry, and my father about you and our bond." Frowning, he grumbled, "I'll have to see how long they give me to vacate my cabin and pride lands."

Germaine opened his mouth, then closed it again. "I was going to ask if your father would speak up for you." He grimaced. "Then I realized how stupid of a question that would have been."

Scoffing, Sage nodded. "Yeah." His expression pensive, he admitted, "I don't even know if my mother will speak up for me once she realizes I'm coming out of the closet."

"I hope she'll still support you," Germaine told him. Trying to lighten the mood, he told him, "And you'll always have the support of my yahoo friends."

Sage chuckled softly. "Dakota does seem like a nice enough guy."

Before Germaine could comment, he heard the trill of Sage's phone . . . again.

With a groan, Sage lifted onto his elbow and reached for the device.

Germaine chuckled. "You're a popular guy, my mate." He saw the way Sage's brows shot up as he perused the screen, then how he nibbled his lips, clearly uncertain. Squeezing Sage's hip, Germaine asked, "Who is it?"

Sage's face took on a pinkish hue as embarrassment seeped into his scent. "Uh, Randy is calling me."

"Who's that?" Germaine asked on reflex, although the

name did sound familiar.

Clearing his throat, Sage told him, "I mentioned him and his partner, Cain. I was friends with them for years before they became, uh—"

"Your fuck buddies," Germaine growled, the pieces clicking into place. While Sage nodded, the phone continued to ring. Making a snap decision, Germaine ordered, "Better answer it then, mate. Time to tell them that you have to go back to just being friends."

Although Sage still looked unconvinced, he nodded. "Okay." He answered the call. "Hey, Randy."

CHAPTER SEVEN

"Hey, hot stuff," Randy greeted in his usual chipper way. "How was dealing with your asshole brother?"

"Uh, I haven't actually done that, yet," Sage admitted. Upon seeing his buddy's name on his phone, thoughts of his brother had been the furthest thing from his mind.

"Really?" Randy hummed. "You sound a little off. Is everything okay? What's wrong?"

Sage sighed deeply as he felt Germaine's arms tighten around him.

"Come back and relax," Germaine crooned into his ear, urging him back to sprawling on his chest. "We're okay." He nipped at Sage's lobe before whispering, "I know what you did with them is in the past, even if I do growl and sound like a possessive asshole."

As Sage sighed again and allowed Germaine to position him back half-sprawled over his chest, he murmured, "Okay."

"Our bond is new," Germaine reminded him before pressing a kiss to Sage's temple. "Talk to your friend."

"Sage?" Randy questioned slowly. "Who's that?" A sensual murmur entered his voice as he pressed, "Did you find someone to hook up with, you sly dog?" Randy's next words came out quieter, even though it was apparent he was shouting. "Cain, come here! Sage hooked up with someone!"

Groaning, Sage shook his head. "I didn't," he countered, feeling his cheeks heat.

Even though Randy and Cain had told him that they didn't

take a third to their bed other than him, they'd always encouraged Sage to find fun where he could. Sage even had a time or two, and the guys had always wanted to know all about it.

"It's not like that," Sage added.

"So, tell us what it's like." That was Cain, and if Sage wasn't mistaken, he was grinning. "Can he hear us?"

"Put your phone on speaker, babe," Germaine ordered.

Sage met Germaine's gaze. "Are you sure? Most men don't want to meet their partner's ex-lovers."

"Just do it, my mate," Germaine encouraged again, tracing his fingertips along Sage's brow. "It'll be fine. I promise. They're your friends, after all." His dark eyes held a wealth of understanding as he added, "And I certainly wasn't celibate before meeting you."

"Yeah, but you're not answering phone calls from your ex-lovers while in bed with me," Sage countered.

Germaine's brows furrowed as his expression turned a little vacant. "I can't say it won't ever happen," he mused slowly. "I've been around for over two centuries, so I suppose there's a possibility we'll run across one."

"Ex-lovers?" Randy cut into their conversation. "Sage? What's going on? Who is that?"

Cain asked the next question. "Did he just call you his mate?" Disbelief rang in his tone.

Randy gasped. "What?"

Sage grimaced as he met Germaine's expression as he put his phone on speaker. "I was going to ease into that," he admitted.

Germaine sighed. "Sorry, Sage."

Relaxing against Germaine's shoulder once more, Sage placed the phone in the middle of his lover's chest. "You know how all of our leaders always tell us that fated mates are always of the opposite sex?" Upon hearing the affirmative noises of his friends, Sage stated, "Well, when I arrived at

Shifter Council Headquarters, I learned that isn't true . . . like, at all."

Silence.

Sage lifted his head and checked his connection. "Guys?" he asked tentatively.

"You've rendered Randy speechless," Cain told him, his own voice sounding a little strained. "Are you, uh, are you saying that Fate will pair a shifter with someone of the same sex?"

Sage knew that the knowledge was rocking his buddies' worlds. The news had done the same to him.

"Yes," Sage replied softly. "Fate pairs people that are compatible. If someone is gay, male or female, why would Fate pair them with someone of the opposite sex?" Sage had always thought it frustratingly unfair. "Those two wouldn't be compatible, so she gives gay people a mate of the same sex instead."

"A-Are you sure?" Randy whispered, his voice a little squeaky.

Sage hoped he wasn't tearing his best friends' relationship apart, but he knew they needed to know the truth. After all, what if one of them stumbled upon their fated mate? What if they turned him away because they didn't understand the truth?

"Yeah, Randy," Sage assured. "I'm sure. I met Germaine, and it pretty much turned my world on its head." Unable to help himself, he scoffed softly as he added, "Imagine my shock when all the guys we ran into started congratulating us. It was crazy."

"Yeah, that sounds crazy," Cain confirmed softly.

"A-And that's who you're with now?" Randy asked.

"Yes," Sage replied.

"Is he good to you?" Cain's voice sounded hard, as if he were going to open a can of whoop-ass if Sage answered in any way other than the affirmative.

"Yes," Sage confirmed. "My mate's name is Germaine Messalla. He's an enforcer for the council, and he's taking good care of me."

Randy snickered, some of his usual vibrancy returning to his tone as he teased, "Oh, I bet he is. Are you in bed with him?" Humming, Randy asked, "What's he look like? Does he have a big dick?"

Sage felt a surge of jealousy that nearly took his breath away. Having never felt such a sensation while talking with Randy—hell, he'd fucked and told with them before—he barely bit back his growl. To his surprise, he heard Germaine's snort as his chest vibrated beneath him.

Frowning at Germaine, Sage grumbled, "Not funny."

"Now you know how I felt," Germaine teased with a wink. "Hello, Randy and Cain. This is Germaine. Yes, we're in bed together, but that's all you're getting out of us."

"That's so mean! You can't say that and then leave us—" Randy began to whine.

"Babe, that's up to them," Cain cut in, chastising gently.

"But—" Randy began again.

"Sorry, Randy," Germaine interrupted. "When a paranormal finds his mate, we get pretty damn possessive, even to the point of being overbearing." There was a clear warning in his tone. "That's why Sage called you ex-lovers. Sage is my mate, and I know it sounds a bit odd, but if either of you were to try to touch me, Sage would try to rip your throats out."

Sage felt his face heat. A mixture of possessive anger, jealousy, and embarrassment swirled through him. Just the idea of either of his ex-lovers touching Germaine in an inappropriate way caused a riot of protective emotions he struggled to control.

"Really?" Randy sounded intrigued.

"Really," Sage confirmed, finding his tongue. "It's such an odd feeling, but it's true and deep, even though I've known

Germaine for less than" — he paused, glancing at the time on his phone — "three hours."

For another moment, silence fell between them all.

Finally, Cain stated, "I'm really happy for you, Sage," although there was a definite hint of sadness in his tone. "Gods, guys. Why would our alphas always tell us we didn't have a fated mate out there?" Just as quickly, Cain said, "Not that I don't love our relationship, Randy."

"It's okay, Cain," Randy replied softly. "I understand. Really, I do." His sigh came through the line, loud and clear. "Everything we've believed for the last eighty years was a lie."

"Maybe they were lied to, too," Germaine offered, obviously trying to reassure them. "We're going to look into it when we come up there."

"Really?" Randy sounded uncertain. "Are you, um, are you certain coming up here is a good idea?"

"You know how your lion pride feels about, well, fags," Cain pointed out bluntly.

Cain and Randy weren't allowed in pride territory. Many lion shifters discriminated against them if they ran across each other while in town. Even Sage was hassled on occasion due to the fact that he was openly friends with them.

"Don't worry," Germaine replied before Sage could. "We won't be alone, and any trouble the inner circle drops on us will be returned back to them ten-fold."

"Okay." Randy cleared his throat, then asked tentatively, "Will we see you when you're here, Sage? We'd like to say goodbye."

Sage didn't counter their assumption, since he knew it was true. He wouldn't be staying part of the pride for much longer. However, he did reassure his buddies that they would always be friends.

"Finding my mate isn't going to change us being pals,

guys," Sage told them. Meeting Germaine's gaze, he smiled. "It just means any Saturday night movie fests will be very different."

Randy snickered, doing his best to hide the sadness Sage could hear, even through the line. "Okay. Fair enough."

"Plus, if you need anything, I have plenty of buddies who are always happy to help out a friend in need," Germaine claimed. "Some are even happier when it involves danger. The more, the better."

Sage's brows shot up, and he stared at Germaine questioningly.

Germaine winked and mouthed, "Later."

Nodding, Sage returned his focus to Randy and Cain. He told his friends a bit more about Germaine and how they'd met. Then Germaine explained about other same-sex fated pairs in the area.

Before Sage knew it, Randy laughed and stated, "Maybe we should move down there, Cain. Lots of gay support and fated mates." A second later, he muttered, "Oh, um, not that I'm looking. I—Oh, gods. Sorry. I—"

"Stop, Randy." The sound of two men kissing came through the line for a few seconds before Cain stated, "I know what you meant." Then Cain told them, "We're gonna let you go, guys. We're both happy for you, Sage. Really."

"Yeah," Randy confirmed, once more subdued. "Be sure to let us know when you're around, okay?"

After Sage confirmed that he would, they said their goodbyes, and the line disconnected.

For several minutes, silence filled the room.

Threading his fingers through Sage's hair, Germaine quietly asked, "Do you think they'll be okay? How long have they been together?"

"I hope they will be," Sage replied. "Um, thirty-three years, I think."

"And they brought you in as an occasional third?"

Sage heard the slight growl in Germaine's tone, but he kept his expression neutral. He nodded.

"Then it's obvious they need more than what they can give each other," Germaine mused. With a sigh, he finished, "I hope they realize that, and should Fate decide to bless one or both of them, they'll help each other cope with those changes." Squeezing Sage's hip, Germaine added, "And we will be there for them, too."

"It's possible they'll stay together and never look for their fated mate," Sage pointed out. He knew the pair could be stubborn, especially Randy.

Germaine grunted even as he nodded. "Problem is, even if they're not looking, Fate could bring their mate to them at any time, so it's good that they have the knowledge to deal with that."

"Yeah," Sage agreed absently, still worrying about his friends.

Fortunately, Germaine's continued petting was beginning to heat his blood, distracting him from his troubles. With his dick plumping, Sage pushed up and rolled on top of his mate. He straddled his lover, pleased to find an answering half-hard cock pressing against his own—and quickly thickening.

A low buzzing noise filled the air.

Arching one brow, Sage smirked at Germaine.

Germaine groaned and rolled his eyes as he reached for his phone.

Sage folded his hands on Germaine's chest and rested his chin upon them. Watching the disappointment and feeling his lover's groan rumble beneath him, he knew they were about to be interrupted by a third phone call in as many hours.

"Damn," Sage grumbled. "It's a miracle we made it through claiming each other."

Sighing, Germaine rubbed up and down Sage's arm. "We'll

get to the slow, exploratory sex soon, my mate. Promise." Then he answered his phone. "Enforcer Germaine."

While Sage easily made out the words of the man speaking, he didn't recognize the male's voice. "I've learned some interesting things from Glade. I understand his brother is with you. Can he hear me?"

Germaine met Sage's gaze. "Yes, he can hear you, Enforcer Malone. You may speak freely."

"Then you may want to take Sage into custody," Enforcer Malone answered bluntly. "Since he's here to help Glade break out of here."

On a growl, Germaine asked, "Does it have to do with the ring? Because Sage has already handed that over to Head Enforcer Mycroft."

"Really?" Malone sounded surprised. "I think I better talk to the boss then. And get Sage ready to meet with his brother. I want to see them interact." Before Germaine could reply, Malone ordered, "Bring him to the interrogation rooms in twenty minutes."

"Yes, Enforcer Malone," Germaine replied. "We'll be there."

Sage watched Germaine disconnect the line. Then his mate smiled at him. "That gives us time to shower. Do you have clean clothes in your *Wagoneer*? I can have someone fetch them for you while we get cleaned up."

Confused, Sage asked, "You don't even want to talk about what Enforcer Malone just told you?"

Germaine urged Sage off the bed as he shrugged. "Why worry about it? I know it's not true, and so does Mycroft." Taking his hand, he tugged him toward the bathroom. "Otherwise, I could give you some sweats and a shirt, but you'll have to roll up the legs."

Sage realized Germaine didn't care one wit about the other enforcer's accusations, so he decided he wouldn't either. "I'd prefer the clothes in my vehicle, please."

Nodding, Germaine headed into the bathroom where Sage had left his stuff. "Give me the keys, then start the shower. I'll get someone to snag your bag" — he smirked as he swept a heated gaze down, then up, Sage's body — "then I'll join you and help you wash your back."

Anticipation heating his blood, Sage nodded. "Okay."

As Germaine took Sage's keys with one hand, he gripped Sage's burgeoning erection with his other.

Sage hissed and rocked his hips when Germaine gave him a light squeeze. His dick filled the rest of the way, and he grabbed his mate's upper arms for support. For several seconds, Germaine massaged his dick as Sage fucked his fist.

"I'm gonna bring the lube, Sage," Germaine claimed, his dark eyes full of heat. "So I can feel this in my ass as you pound me into the shower wall."

Groaning, Sage nodded. "Please."

"Hell, yeah." Then Germaine and the exquisite pressure was gone.

Sage groaned in disappointment, and it took him several long, slow deep breaths to get enough self-control to move enough to start the shower water.

CHAPTER EIGHT

As Germaine glanced down at a sleeping Sage in his arms, he appreciated how swift the meeting with the man's brother had turned out.

Glade had stared defiantly at them all, then scowled at Sage. "It's about time you showed up," he'd snapped. Then he'd peered imperiously around at everyone in the room—Germaine, Malone, and Gierson, a black panther shifter and fellow enforcer. "I want to talk to my brother alone."

"Is that what you want, Sage?" Germaine had asked, cocking his head. No way in hell had he wanted to leave his mate alone with his asshole brother, but when Sage had nodded once, he'd done it. "Hit this button when you're ready." He'd pointed at a buzzer beside the door. Then he'd added, "Otherwise, we'll be back in ten minutes."

Unbeknownst to the standard enforcer—and even most councilmen—everything said in the interrogation rooms was recorded. Everyone had filed into the viewing room attached to the interrogation room. As it had happened, Germaine had heard Glade demand the ring.

"I wasn't allowed to bring it in here," Sage had told Glade. "Head Enforcer Mycroft said he would keep it locked up until your sentence was completed."

"That's not standard procedure," Glade had snarled, leaning over the table toward Sage. Even sitting down and chained to the table, the lion shifter made an intimidating image. "You shouldn't have allowed that."

Sage had leaned back in his seat in an obvious attempt to

put space between them. "I didn't know that." He'd hunched his shoulders and muttered, "Not like I could go against him."

"Just wait until Father hears," Glade had snarled, a malicious light filling his hazel eyes. "Wish I'd be around to see that." Then Glade had waved his hand imperiously. "Get out of here, loser. You're no good to me."

Germaine had glanced between his fellow enforcers, not at all pleased by the exchange. He'd known he hadn't been the only one thinking they would have to keep a close eye on Bill and Glade Kanston. His gut had told him something else was going on.

"How's he doing?"

Hearing Investigator Ryzer Dialnist's soft question, Germaine smiled at the shifter sitting in the middle seat of the SUV.

Ryzer had dyed neon green streaks into his brown hair. He'd switched out his piercings from the last time Germaine had seen him. Instead of four black studs with three tiny silver hoops running up his left ear, he had one stud for every color of the rainbow — in order starting at the top — red, orange, yellow, green, blue, indigo, and violet. Ryzer also sported painted on, deep-colored orange jeans, an indigo form-fitting polo shirt, light make-up on his face, and bright blue nails.

Anyone walking down the street would peg the five-foot-seven-inch man as a flaming queen.

In truth, Germaine didn't actually know what the man's orientation was, or if he considered himself anything at all.

"He's okay," Germaine told the much smaller shifter. "Resting comfortably."

Enforcer Dakota drove the SUV while Enforcer Gierson rode shotgun, allowing him and Sage to cuddle up in the back. His mate had originally talked about driving his own vehicle, but he'd convinced his mate that they needed something bigger and more intimidating to make an entrance. Also, Enforcer Austin, a water buffalo shifter, followed them in a pick-up truck . . . just in case Sage needed to pack up his cabin immediately. Otherwise, the enforcer would stay out of sight, acting as a tourist in town.

"Can't be easy to have your brother call you a loser," Ryzer commented, rubbing his fingers over his piercings. "Always thought that guy was an overbearing asshole."

Germaine nodded in agreement as he grimaced. "He said he's been called that and worse, so he didn't think anything of it."

"Dickwad," Ryzer muttered, shaking his head.

"We're coming up on Boston," Dakota stated from the front. "Sunrise is in an hour, and we should be at the edge of pride lands about then, too."

They'd driven through the night, so they could drop in first thing on the alpha and his inner circle.

"How much notice are we giving them?" Gierson asked, mild amusement filling his tone. "Or none at all?"

"Well, we want them all there," Ryzer mused. "Got any idea what time those of the alpha-house normally eat breakfast?"

From Sage's information, Alpha Colton and Beta Larry both lived at the main house, as did an enforcer named Mitch. There was also a live-in chef named Ingra, Colton's daughter, Meribeth, and a low-level enforcer named Truman, who also acted as the butler.

"Seven-thirty," Sage mumbled, revealing he was awake. He shifted his head where he had it resting on Germaine's shoulder so he could peer forward. "Alpha Colton has his first cup of coffee at seven with his inner circle. No one is to disturb them. My father always joins them. He eats breakfast with them, too, but always returns for lunch with Mother at eleven-thirty and dinner at six." Sage paused to yawn deeply, then finished, "Unless there's an emergency, everyone knows never to interrupt meal times. It's also supposed to be an honor to be invited, although I never have been."

"Even though you're the head enforcer's son?" Gierson asked, turning to peer back at them.

Sage pushed off Germaine and sat up straight. "Hell, no," he replied with a scoff. "I'm not the big buff lion shifter like Glade. I don't even know if my mom's ever been, either." Sage appeared speculative for a moment. "Although, that could be because she always had me to prepare a meal for while growing up. Maybe she does now."

"Well, we'll see in a couple of hours, then," Dakota replied glibly, grinning into the rearview mirror at them. "Should we stop at a hotel to get cleaned up first?"

"Gods, yes," Sage replied with another yawn. "And coffee."

Everyone laughed as they agreed.

Less than three hours later, they were all back in the SUV. They'd all showered and dressed in more formal clothing. Dakota, Gierson, and Germaine had donned black dress slacks, charcoal gray polo shirts, and black sports coats. Sage had chosen navy blue dress slacks, a dark-blue button-down, and his coat.

Not surprisingly, Ryzer was the odd man out, although he still looked pretty snappy. He had chosen a pair of pale-blue slacks, a deep yellow dress shirt, and a neon green jacket. His streaked hair was styled to perfection, as was his make-up and lipstick.

Within fifteen minutes of leaving the hotel, they were on pride property. The area became increasingly rural, with green-treed rolling hills and plenty of small bridges over rivers and streams. The fresh, forested scent permeated the SUV, even beating out the aroma of their coffees.

Germaine had found it interesting that Ryzer had declined coffee in favor of green tea.

Weird guy.

"The road the alpha's house is on is to the left," Sage told them, pointing.

Dakota dutifully turned.

In less than five minutes, Sage stated, "That's the driveway on the right. Fifty-two-oh-six is on the mailbox."

"Can't see the house from the road," Gierson mused. "Smart for a shifter pride lodge." Turning in his seat, he asked Sage, "Are most of the houses we passed on this road occupied by shifters?"

"Anything within three miles of here is shifter owned, then the percentage goes down from there," Sage explained. "My pride has an in at almost every real estate company in the area, so we always have advance notice if humans in the area decide to sell."

"What about you, Sage? Where is your cottage from here?" Ryzer asked, beating Germaine to the question.

Sage pointed to the north. "I'm to the north. About seven miles from where our territory abuts against Alpha Brenner's fox territory."

"Can't wait to see it," Germaine claimed with a wink. "You got a fireplace in it?"

Sage's green eyes began to darken. "Sure do."

The way he looked at Germaine and the scent beginning to fill the back of the SUV told him that his mate had a few ideas on how to enjoy that fireplace together.

Ryzer chuckled. "Bank the arousal, boys," he teased. "We're here."

Just that fast, Sage's scent of desire was replaced by one of nerves.

"Relax, my mate," Germaine rumbled, squeezing his mate's neck. "All will be well."

"Gods, I sure hope so," Sage mumbled, not sounding at all convinced. He glanced around at everyone as the vehicle came to a stop. "I don't want anyone to get hurt."

Dakota snorted as he shut off the engine. "If he dares hurt any of us, he'll bring so much heat from the council down on his head." He smirked as he peered over his shoulder at Sage. "Not to mention from my brothers."

Germaine had explained that the man they'd given crap to in the elevator—Enforcer Dane—was Dakota's other older brother. Delanrue was the oldest and was the enforcer Glade had wronged. Germaine had found out later that Dane had been in the process of escorting Councilman Colearian and Theo to Mycroft's office to get the investigation into Sage's pride started as swiftly as possible.

"It's now or never," Ryzer stated with a snicker. "Let's go have some *fun*."

While the others chuckled, Germaine noticed Sage did not. "You ready, my mate?" he asked him softly as doors opened and clothing rustled as the others exited.

Sage tucked his nose into the crook near Germaine's armpit. After inhaling deeply, obviously taking comfort from his scent, he straightened. Although his smile appeared a little forced, Sage nodded.

"Let's go, handsome," Germaine urged, touching the small of his back.

Germaine watched as Sage eased out of the back of the SUV. He knew Ryzer would be right there to keep an eye on Sage, as would Gierson. That gave him the opportunity to slide slowly from the vehicle, keeping up the appearance of detached confidence.

Once out of the SUV, Germaine took a few seconds to straighten his jacket. That gave him time to inhale and exhale, taking in the scents. He also panned his gaze around the area, getting the lay of the land as best he could in that short time.

"All right then," Dakota rumbled. "Let's head up to the door and knock." He looked at the panther enforcer. "Gierson, please lead the way."

Although Germaine technically had more seniority, giving him a slight edge in shifter enforcer hierarchy, he was freshly mated to Sage. That meant his focus would be on his tiger and his happiness. Dakota would take point on their operation to keep an unbiased decision-maker in charge — to the best of his ability, anyway.

While Dakota was a good man, a fair man, he also had a healthy dislike for bigots and bullies.

Personally, Germaine appreciated that about him.

Resting his hand on the small of Sage's back, Germaine urged him to fall into step behind Dakota. Ryzer fell into step to Dakota's right, flanking him. The small shifter sauntered more than strode, his chin up and a haughty expression on his face, clearly comfortable with himself.

The sound of Gierson's bold knock thundered through the early morning air.

They didn't have long to wait.

The door opened to reveal a scowling, dark-haired man. His eyes narrowed as he swept over them. When his focus snagged on Sage, he curled his lip for an instant before clearing his expression.

Dakota lifted his chin. "Good morning. I'm Council Enforcer Dakota Delanrue. I'm here to speak with Alpha Colton Bruwer."

The man glanced Sage's way again before refocusing on Dakota and saying, "Is he expecting you?"

Curving his lips into a cold smile, Dakota stated, "You already know the answer to that, Enforcer Truman."

While the man didn't respond verbally, his scent gave away his surprise that Dakota knew who he was.

"I advise you to invite us in," Dakota suggested.

Truman's nostrils flared, and it was damn obvious that he wanted to refuse. Instead, he tipped his chin in the faintest of nods. Then he swung the door wider and took a step backward.

Pointing to the left, Truman stated, "Please wait in the sitting room." He again glanced at Sage before adding, "I'll tell Alpha Colton that you're here."

Gierson moved first, leading the way into the home, making it obvious that he was scouting the interior. Dakota followed, with Ryzer flanking him. The mouse shifter glanced at Truman for only an instant before dismissing him and looking around the room.

With his hand on Sage's lower back, Germaine followed at the back. He spotted the way Truman peered at Ryzer with a curled lip of distaste. The big lion shifter scoffed under his breath, which was plenty loud enough for all of them to hear, before stalking deeper into the house.

In the front room, Sage opened his mouth, but Dakota lifted his finger to his lips, silently shushing him. He softened the order by winking. Then the komodo dragon shifter headed to a large chair and sprawled in it.

Germaine guided Sage to the love seat nearby, and both of them took a seat. Gierson stood behind Dakota. Ryzer, on the other hand, wandered around the room, touching everything, and making adjustments to how they were placed.

Sage's eyes were huge in his face as he watched, and Gierson's lips twitched. They all knew exactly what he was doing—baiting the alpha. Would the lion shifter be rude to council representatives, even an openly flaming one, about something so trivial as to how the knick-knacks on the fireplace mantel were placed? Or was he smart enough to see it as the test it was and ignore it?

Germaine had to admit that he was curious to see what would happen.

The thud of boots reached them, telling them that the inner circle were joining them long before the men actually showed up. Truman arrived first and moved to the left of the door. He spotted several other men that he recognized from pictures on Sage's phone — Alpha Colton, Beta Larry, Enforcer Mitch, and of course, Enforcer Bill.

Sage's father took three steps into the room before he growled. He cast an angry look Sage's way before peering around at the others. Crossing his arms over his chest, Bill curled his lip and asked, "What the hell has my good for nothing son done now?"

Germaine felt Sage stiffen next to him, and it took every bit of his self-control not to jump across the room and layout the asshole enforcer. The man had called Sage similar things and more when his mate had called to give a short recount of how his meeting with Glade had gone. To say Bill had been furious about the loss of his ring had been . . . an understatement.

After this, somehow, I will never allow him to harm my mate again — verbally or otherwise.

CHAPTER NINE

Sage did his best to hide the cringe, but he figured Germaine could feel it. The tick that appeared in the slender black male's jaw combined with how he narrowed his eyes just a little gave it away. Doing his best to ignore his father's hatred and his mate's protectiveness, Sage kept his mouth shut as he listened to Dakota answer.

He would never admit it to anyone, but he was damn glad he didn't have to hold this conversation with his father alone. *And now I barely have to add much to the conversation at all.*

"Good for nothing?" Dakota repeated, arching one blond eyebrow. "It's too bad you feel that way, because Fate certainly doesn't."

"What's that supposed to mean?" his father demanded, seeming to completely forget that with Alpha Colton in the room, he wasn't supposed to be the one doing the talking. "He's a pansy-assed helper at a candy store." Scoffing, his father curved his lip in derision. "How is that good for anything?"

Evidently, Alpha Colton was done allowing his enforcer to usurp his authority — if only he knew. "That's enough, Enforcer Bill," he stated, holding up his hand.

Although Bill snapped his mouth shut, his eyes remained narrowed, expressing his disdain.

"I'm Alpha Colton. My apologies for Enforcer Bill's actions, Enforcer Dakota," Alpha Colton said as he stepped forward. "It seems a family squabble has broken out, but we'll handle that internally." Turning his attention to Sage, the alpha ordered, "You can head home now, Sage. I'll contact you this afternoon with an appointment time to discuss whatever you are here for."

Then Alpha Colton moved toward the fireplace with Beta Larry following him. "I'm certain you're aware this is my beta, Larry." He pointed toward the doorway. "My other enforcers, Mitch and Truman."

Colton took a few seconds to adjust a large iron horse on the mantel, returning it to the position it'd been in before Ryzer had moved it.

"Why aren't you moving, boy?" Enforcer Bill demanded. "The alpha said to go."

Sage had been too stunned at seeing his father silenced to think about moving. He had very little experience with the inner circle of his pride. Staying on the outskirts, flying below the radar, had always been in his best self-interest.

Guess that's changing now.

Opening his mouth, Sage wondered how he should respond . . . and to whom.

Fortunately, Dakota beat him to the punch once more. "Sage must stay," the big enforcer stated. Appearing relaxed in the large chair, he stretched out his legs and crossed them at the ankles. "He's one of the reasons we're here today." His smile stretched across his features but didn't reach his green eyes. "Thank you for sending Sage to inquire about Glade. That action allowed Fate to work her magic."

Before Bill could comment, Alpha Colton turned his attention to his enforcer. "You sent Sage to Council Headquarters without telling me? Why?" His scowl appeared fierce and full of annoyance. "And what's going on with Glade? Is his vacation delayed?"

"And why does he keep talking about Fate?" Beta Larry muttered under his breath.

For just an instant, Sage thought his father looked like a

deer caught in the headlights. It certainly wasn't a look he'd ever expected to see on the man. He'd always been put together and forceful . . . or vicious.

Ingra appeared in the doorway pushing a tray, saving Sage's father. "Sorry for the interruption, Alpha," she stated. "Here's the coffee service you requested."

To Sage's surprise, his mother followed Ingra into the room pushing another tray. "And the pastries." Her gaze fell on Sage, and her face lit up. "Sage, darling! I didn't know you were back in town."

Disregarding all sense of hierarchy or propriety, his mother rushed across the room and grabbed Sage, pulling him to his feet. She wrapped him in a tight hug, rocking him from side to side, and Sage had little choice but to return the embrace. Besides, he'd always loved his mother's hugs.

Then Mary Kanston eased her hold and took a step back. "Let me look at you," she murmured, resting her hands on Sage's shoulders. Mary grinned, her green eyes — so similar to his own — lit up. "My, but you look good. Did everything go okay in Savannah?" Just as quickly, she glanced around and realized everyone was staring at them with various expressions, and she blanched. "Um, we'll discuss that later, dear. Why don't you head to our place, and I'll be along shortly to make you some breakfast." She released him, as if that alone would get him moving. "It's so early. I'm sure you haven't eaten yet."

"It's good to see you, too, Mom," Sage told her, finding his tongue. "But I can't leave yet." Upon seeing his mother's brows furrow in concern, he quickly added, "Enforcer Dakota will explain."

Sage didn't like how his mother wrung her hands, but he couldn't do anything else to reassure her. When Germaine rose and gripped his elbow, he turned to his mate. His lover smiled and urged him back to the sofa, joining him there. Germaine slung his arm across the back of the furniture, and Sage barely resisted cuddling up to his side.

While that had been going on, Ingra had been serving coffee and tea to the others. His mother quickly joined her, wheeling the pastry cart around and between seats. Once everyone was settled with coffee and food — Sage had chosen an apple turnover while Germaine picked a raspberry jelly donut — Alpha Colton focused on Dakota.

"Okay, Enforcer Dakota," Alpha Colton began after taking a sip of his tea. "My apologies for the odd beginning to your unexpected visit." His smile turned ingratiating. "Let's begin again. Shall we?"

"Of course, Alpha Colton," Dakota replied with a calm-looking smile. "Allow me to introduce the rest of my party." Once that was done, he continued, "We felt the changes in life affecting your enforcer's sons was something we should share in person."

Alpha Colton nodded once. "Very well. As you probably ascertained, I was not made aware that Enforcer Bill's younger son had been sent to Shifter Headquarters to see Glade."

"Is it so odd that Sage would want to visit with his older brother?" Ryzer piped up from where he leaned his hip on a sideboard. He'd been introduced as an enforcer rather than an investigator. After asking his question, he arched one thin brow and sipped his green tea.

Sage had been surprised Ingra had the beverage available.

Alpha Colton flicked his gaze over Ryzer, his lips pinching, expressing his distaste. "First, I was under the impression that Sage and Council Enforcer Glade don't run in the same circles. Second, he's scheduled to visit the pride in a couple of months, so a pop-in visit from Sage would be completely out of character." Colton focused on Sage. "Why did you go to headquarters, and why wasn't I informed that you'd be out of the territory for an extended length of time?"

Shifting uncomfortably in his seat, Sage forced his gaze to remain on the alpha's collarbone. He didn't want his alpha to think he was challenging his cat. Plus, no way did Sage want to see the kind of look his father would give him since he had every intention of answering honestly.

"My father told me about a report that came through email, how Glade got himself into some hot water," Sage told his alpha, choosing his words carefully. "Father ordered me to go to headquarters to see just how bad it was and if there was any way we could help him." Clearing his throat, he met his alpha's gaze and admitted, "There's nothing we can do at this time, so Glade won't be here like we'd originally thought."

"I see," Alpha Colton replied with a distinctive chill in his voice. He pinned a hard look on Enforcer Bill while saying, "We will discuss certain aspects of *that* later." Then he refocused on Dakota. "Why was having Sage at Council Headquarters a good thing with Fate? Is my pride member helping our leaders in some way?"

"Well, Sage was able to share information that is helping us," Dakota began, tipping his head to the side. "But that's not what Fate's blessing is." Curving his lips into a wide grin, he finally revealed, "Sage found his fated mate while at Council Headquarters."

"What!" Sage's mother shrieked, her pleasure obvious in the way she clapped her hands together. "Who is she?" She rushed back across the room. "Where is she?" She stopped beside the sofa with her hands clasped together before her breasts as she bounced on her toes. "When can I meet her?"

"You can meet *him* now," Dakota replied, rising to his feet. "After all, he's sitting right next to Sage." Moving closer to the pair, as did the others, Dakota stated into the clearly shocked silence—even Sage's mother had stopped bouncing with excitement and stared with wide eyes—while indicating Germaine. "This is Council Enforcer Germaine Messalla. He's Sage's fated mate."

Germaine rose, so Sage did the same.

Holding out his hand, Germaine stated, "It's nice to meet you, Sage's mom." He grinned as he added, "You've raised a fine son. I'm so proud Fate has paired him with me." Finally, Sage's mother reached out and took Germaine's hand, and his mate continued, "It's my honor to take care of him, just as I know he'll do for me."

Confusion rolling from her scent, Sage's mother glanced from Sage to Germaine, then around at the inner circle who were still staring in silence and sporting various expressions—from shocked to confusion to disbelief to disgust. The last one, of course, was Bill.

"But, I don't understand," she began hesitantly, tugging her hand away. "I didn't think Fate paired those of the same sex."

"They don't," Sage's father barked belligerently. "This is bullshit, a lie, a farce." Curling his lip, he stalked forward enough to grab his mate and pull her away from the group. He pinned a hate-filled gaze on Sage. "Are you telling me you're a faggot? This is how you decide to do it? With lies to embarrass me in front of our alpha?"

The enforcer's voice rose with each word he spoke until he was practically yelling.

Enforcer Gierson stepped between Sage, Germaine, and the irate lion shifter. "I'm going to ask you to please step backward, Enforcer Bill," he ordered, lifting a hand with his palm out. "And please calm down. Your son is not lying." The black panther shifter's dark eyes narrowed as his tone took on a warning quality. "Nor is Enforcer Dakota or Enforcer Germaine."

To Sage's relief, Beta Larry stepped forward and gripped his father's upper arm. "Our apologies, enforcers," he stated diplomatically as he tugged Sage's father backward a few steps. His father's hold on his mother assured that she would go with him. Larry offered a tight smile Dakota's way. "I'm certain our enforcer in no way meant that you were lying. It seems there has been a misunderstanding, however."

Enforcer Dakota nodded sagely. "Indeed, there *has* been a misunderstanding." He turned and addressed Alpha Colton. "Sage told us about how your pride and the nearby fox skulk hold the belief that Fate did not pair those of the same sex." His chuckle sounded a little rueful as he glanced Sage's way with a small smile. "Poor Sage had quite the time wrapping his head around the fact that Germaine was his mate, especially when we all started congratulating him." Dakota patted Sage on the back once, appearing jovial, as if trying to lighten the situation. Sobering, Dakota returned his attention to the alpha. "Another reason the council chose to send representatives with Sage and Enforcer Germaine was to talk to you all about this misinformation that seems to continue pervading our people. Fate *does* pair those of the same sex. Where did this belief come from? Is it just an outdated notion that has been passed down over the centuries? Or did it show up in a report from the Shifter Council somewhere?" Dakota smiled. "We really need to get to the bottom of this."

Enforcer Mitch scratched the back of his neck. "Soooo, Fate pairs those of the same sex?"

To Sage, the big man actually looked . . . hopeful.

Enforcer Dakota nodded with a grin. "She sure does."

"Huh," Mitch muttered, staring at the floor.

CHAPTER TEN

Germaine walked down the small town street, his fingers twined with Sage's. As much as he loved holding his mate's hand, he wished he could help ease the man's nerves. He noticed the way Sage would glance around furtively, as if waiting for someone to say something derogatory to him.

While Germaine hadn't intended to thrust Sage out of the closet, he hadn't actually realized his mate was *in* the closet, either. Sage had always been so open with him about being gay. When they'd been at Shifter Headquarters, he'd always welcomed Germaine's touch.

He was finding that out in town was a completely different story.

"I'm sorry if I'm making you uncomfortable," Germaine murmured, feeling the tension in the arm beside him. "Should I release your hand?" As Germaine spoke, he began to loosen his fingers, intending to do just that.

"No," Sage snapped, scowling. He immediately softened his expression into a small smile as he shook his head. "No, I really like holding your hand." Pausing on the sidewalk, Sage admitted, "I've just never demonstrated my orientation like this before. It just makes me a little nervous."

"Do you mind telling me why?" Germaine began reaching for Sage's face with his free hand, but he stayed the action. They were in the middle of the sidewalk, after all. "Is it because you think someone from your pride will be around to harass you?"

Sage nodded, nibbling his bottom lip. "Yeah." Grimacing,

he muttered, "I'm sure my being gay is making the rounds of the pride like wildfire."

"Who would tell the others?"

Germaine couldn't help but be curious. Most of the people in the meeting had been from headquarters or the pride's inner circle. The others had been Sage's mother and the chef, who Sage had told him was named Ingra. Germaine couldn't imagine that Enforcer Bill would allow his wife to tell anyone, and if Ingra was a blabber-mouth, no way would she have ended up the chef to the alpha.

"Um, well—" Sage frowned for a second before smiling wanly at him. "I can't think of anyone."

Chuckling, Germaine tugged on Sage's hand and started them moving again. "Come on. Stop worrying so much and show me where you work." He couldn't wait to check out all the sweets and candy that Sage had told him about. As they started walking again, Germaine added, "And if you're too concerned, you should know that's Austin sitting at that outdoor table across the street."

Sage followed Germaine's discreet indication. "That's the water buffalo shifter enforcer, right?"

Germaine nodded. "It is. He's a good man, and if you run into a problem, he'll be around. He's watching our backs since we're in town alone," he admitted. Just because he felt certain he could handle any problems himself didn't mean he wasn't going to have help lined up . . . just in case.

"Okay," Sage replied dubiously. "He looks a little . . . scary."

Chuckling softly, Germaine nodded. "That he does." That had been the plan, too.

Austin stood a solid six-foot-five, had wide shoulders and a massive torso, and heavily muscled tree-trunks for legs. His medium-brown hair hung in thick waves to his shoulders, and his goatee nearly hid full lips. When Austin wasn't wearing his sunglasses, his dark eyes held a solemn, penetrating quality.

Germaine knew that some of that was caused by sadness. When the crimes perpetrated by a pair of councilmen came to light, some enforcers backed them, helping them escape. They'd all been named rogue, and a discreet battle had commenced.

Austin's two middle brothers—Gaston and Ephram—had joined the rogues' ranks. They'd eventually been caught and put to death for their crimes after they'd tried to murder another councilman and his mate. While Austin had a third brother—Bran, the youngest—they'd always been estranged, although Germaine had never heard way.

Perhaps their mutual loss will help them mend broken fences.

The dinging of a shop bell followed by Sage tugging on Germaine's hand drew him out of his thoughts. He hadn't even stepped through the door of Ellen's Sweet Shop before the smell of sugar assailed his nostrils. Just inside the door, he took in the myriad of colorful confectionary delights.

"Damn," Germaine mumbled in awe. "This place is . . ." He wasn't even certain how to describe it.

"Awesome," Sage finished with a chuckle. "The word you're looking for is awesome."

Germaine laughed softly. "Totally. It's like something out of *Willie Wonka and Chocolate Factory*," he commented as he began strolling around the place, staring at all the choices.

While the shop was only a single story, the way the candy-filled dispensers went nearly to the ceiling made it seem bigger. Those lined the outer walls. Little shelves between them were filled with small brown paper sacks and pens. That allowed someone to write the item number on the brown paper sack, place the open mouth of the bag under the dispenser's spout, and pour the desired amount in there.

Underneath them were large plastic bins filled with different kinds of sweets—from taffy to gummies to cinnamon bears and more. Each of those had small individual scoops to use to fill a bag. There were scales available to weigh the bags between every fourth or fifth dispenser.

The middle table ran the entire length of the store and contained individually wrapped bars of all different sorts. At the back of the store was a long bar with glass cases underneath. These were filled with fudges and chocolate-covered fruits. The attendant would need to help with them as well as the myriad of licorice ropes and sweet tabs plus a few other odds and ends kept back there.

"Here."

Germaine yanked his gaze from the offered items and focused on Sage. His mate was holding up a pair of latex gloves. Taking them, he arched a brow in silent question.

"For cleanliness," Sage explained. He pointed at a glove dispenser. "No one can touch the candy if they aren't wearing a pair, and those who work here always put a pair on if they leave behind the counter."

Germaine realized there was a glove dispenser on either side of the door as well as either end of the long table. Taking the gloves, he dutifully put them on. As he did so, he asked, "How do they monitor that?"

Sage pulled on his own gloves, then pointed at the corner. "The floor behind the counter is raised about eight inches higher than the main store," he explained. "That way, with the mirrors, we can keep an eye on everything going on in here."

"Sage! Welcome back," an older woman greeted as she headed around the table toward them. She was grinning broadly at Sage as she closed the distance. "It's never the same without you. Did you have a good trip?"

"Hi, Misses Ellen," Sage replied before accepting a hug from the woman. "I did have a good trip. Thanks." After he'd stepped backward, his cheeks took on a slightly ruddy glow as he indicated Germaine. "This is Germaine. He's, um, he's my boyfriend."

Misses Ellen's brows shot up, but only for an instant. Then she grinned broadly as she took off the rubber gloves she'd been wearing. She offered her right hand, so Germaine followed her actions and did the same, clasping her's in a gentle hold.

"Nice to meet you, Germaine," Misses Ellen told him, and from her pleased scent, he knew she truly was.

"Same to you, Misses Ellen," Germaine replied. "Sage has only good things to say about you and your amazing shop." He grinned broadly as he claimed, "I couldn't miss checking it out while I was in town."

"Oh, Sage is always a sweet young man," Misses Ellen gushed. "Are you moving here to be with him?"

Germaine fought back a smile at her nosiness and decided to take advantage and told her, "Actually, I'm trying to convince him to move to Savannah to be with me." He kept his tone apologetic even as he revealed, "I can't see myself without him, you see."

Misses Ellen sighed as she nodded. "I always knew it would just be a matter of time before some handsome man swept him off his feet." Then her nose wrinkled as she tittered. Patting Germaine's hand, she stated, "Well, to be honest, I thought it would be some sweet young woman, but I can certainly see the appeal of you. Tall, dark, and handsome." Misses Ellen winked largely before turning her focus to Sage and laughing a bit more when she patted his cheek. "Oh, look at you. It's so good to see you with someone." The store's bell jingled, and she glanced beyond them for a second. With a smile, she told them, "Let me know if you boys need anything."

Then Misses Ellen pulled on her gloves and greeted the other customer.

For the next thirty minutes, Sage stuck close to Germaine's side as he wandered around the store. He couldn't help but be impressed with the massive assortment of goodies available. There was everything from chocolate bars to peanut brittle to chocolate-covered strawberries.

Sage had told him those last items were made by the deli Austin had been sitting at every morning. They usually sold out by lunch, so Germaine bought the last two. He also picked up a box of candy-coated black licorice — relieved to find Sage would eat them, too — a long, red licorice rope, and a large bag of cinnamon bears.

"Like the chewy stuff, do you?" Sage teased as he eyed Germaine's choices. He'd been in talking to Misses Ellen while Germaine had been ringing up his purchases. "Not big on salty?"

Germaine growled softly as he thought of something salty that he loved oh-so-much. While he'd been all for heading straight to Sage's cabin to enjoy just that kind of treat, Sage had wanted to show him the town. When his mate had told him that he was going to give a verbal notice to Misses Ellen, too, he was all for it.

"I like salty just fine," Germaine crooned, bending to whisper into his ear. "I'm pretty sure I proved that last night."

Exhausting Sage by sucking him off, then fucking him through the mattress, was quickly becoming one of Germaine's favorite past times. He intended to do it as often as possible.

To Germaine's pleasure, Sage's cheeks turned a bit pink.

Germaine barely refrained from kissing Sage right there in

the middle of the store. Then he realized something else. Few people would appreciate watching some random strangers make out — even if it was a man and a woman — but that didn't mean he couldn't express his affection another way.

Bending lower, Germaine bussed a kiss to Sage's temple before whispering, "Let's go across the street and get a bite to eat. Then we'll head to your cabin, and I'll prove it all over again."

Hearing Sage's breathing hitch, Germaine straightened before he did something inappropriate. He rested his hand on the small of his mate's back. Guiding him to the door, he reached beyond him to open it for him.

Germaine pointed toward the deli that Austin had been sitting in front of. While the water buffalo shifter was no longer there, he knew the enforcer wouldn't have strayed too far. After receiving a nod from Sage, they headed that way.

As they walked, Germaine took several deep breaths, clearing his lungs of the overly sweet scents that had pervaded the candy shop. "How long have you worked for Misses Ellen?" he asked once he could differentiate between smells again.

"About four years," Sage told him.

"Wow. I don't know how you still have a sense of smell," Germaine commented with a chuckle. "That store definitely had a strong odor."

Sage chuckled. "Yeah, that's a nice way to put it." With a shrug, he told him, "I guess I just got used to it."

Germaine glanced both ways, then started them across the street. They were halfway across when a dark sedan came screeching around the corner fifty feet away. The engine revved as it barreled toward them.

Gasping, Germaine grabbed Sage around the waist and lunged. They hit the sidewalk hard, but he ignored it in favor of using their momentum to roll them even further. He noticed the wheels popping up onto the sidewalk as the vehicle skidded past them.

Panting softly, Germaine continued to cover Sage's body with his own as he peered around the area. He saw several people converging on them, concerned expressions on their faces. One of them was Austin, who had a phone to his ear.

Once the other shifter reached them, Germaine eased off of Sage. "Are you okay?" he asked as he rose to his knees. He did a visual inspection but couldn't see much except a tear in his mate's blue slacks and a dirt scuff on his jacket elbow.

"Yeah, I'm okay," Sage told him, rolling to his ass. His mate took the offered hand of some guy and was pulled to his feet, so Germaine quickly scrambled up, too. Evidently, Sage knew the guy, for he commented, "Thanks, Petre."

"You okay, Sage?" Petre asked, glancing between them. "What about you, man?"

Germaine finally registered Petre's scent and took in cat shifter. "Just a bruise or two," he told the guy. Glancing around at the others, he offered their concerned crowd a reassuring smile. "Nothing a hot bath full of *Epsom* salts won't cure."

One of the women nodded sagely. "Use the ones with eucalyptus scent. So relaxing."

A different woman instantly concurred. "Oh, those are my favorite."

Within thirty seconds, Germaine and Sage were forgotten as the pair began discussing their favorite bath salts and when they liked to use them. Most of the crowd dispersed. Austin, Petre, and a guy wearing a badge on his belt remained.

"I'm Deputy Convers," the human claimed, holding out his hand. "Are you certain you're both okay? Do either of you want to get checked out by a medic?"

Germaine quickly shook his head, Sage doing the same. "Just bumps and bruises," he repeated. Focusing on Sage, he took his lover's hand. "What about you, babe?"

Sage shook his head, squeezing Germaine's hand. "No, I'm okay . . . thanks to you." Frowning, he took the deputy's hand for a few seconds, then released it. "It really looked like that car was aiming for us."

"Yeah, it did," Deputy Convers confirmed. "I only caught a partial plate. What about you guys?" He had a note pad and pen in hand, glancing between them expectantly.

"Yeah, I can tell you," Austin grumbled, finally putting his phone into his pocket. Then he rumbled off the plate.

"And you are?" the deputy asked, looking Austin up and down distrustfully.

"This is Austin O'Malley," Germaine supplied. "He's a friend. We were meeting him at the deli for lunch."

While Petre's brow twitched, betraying that he'd caught the scent of Germaine's lie, the cat shifter didn't call him on it. Instead, he shoved his hands into his pockets and squinted at the pair. His gaze also dropped to their twined fingers a couple of times.

After giving all the information they could — which wasn't much — the deputy moved on, saying he would be in touch.

Once the human was out of earshot, Petre obviously couldn't contain his curiosity any longer. "Does Alpha Colton know you're a couple?" he asked softly. "Because I know your dad's a bigoted ass, Sage. You need to be careful."

"You really shouldn't say that about our head enforcer," Sage cautioned, worry filling his green eyes. "It's true, but I wouldn't want you in trouble for saying it."

"And the whole inner circle knows," Germaine told him. "Can't say how most of them feel, but you're right about Sage's dad." Shaking his head, he muttered, "I sure hope it wasn't him driving that car because it'll get him into deeper hot water. Coming between fated mates is a death sentence, and I'd hate to see something happen to his mother because of his bigotry."

While Germaine had received the distinct impression that Alpha Colton and Beta Larry weren't pleased with the knowledge that Fate paired those of the same sex, they hadn't acted disgusted the way Enforcer Bill and Enforcer Truman had. Enforcer Mitch, on the other hand, had seemed intrigued.

"Wait, did you say fated mate?" Petre asked, confusion clouding his expression. "But I thought—"

"I thought that, too," Sage cut in, a wry smile curving his lips. "But we'd been misinformed." He smiled up at Germaine adoringly. "Trust me."

Germaine really liked that look on Sage's face.

CHAPTER ELEVEN

Sage led Germaine into the home he'd owned for the last twenty-three years. At that time, he'd reinvented his identity, so the first ten years he'd lived there in near seclusion. The only people he'd seen had been his parents, a few pride members, and Randy and Cain.

As Sage showed Germaine around his two-bedroom home, his thoughts turned to his friends. He'd left a message that morning that he was back in town for a little while. To his surprise, he still hadn't heard from them.

I hope they're okay.

"This is a lovely space," Germaine told him, taking his hand. "This fireplace is gorgeous."

"Thanks." Sage smiled up at his mate. "I was thinking, maybe I could keep it as a vacation home?"

"Damn good idea," Germaine replied. His focus slid to the large fireplace. When his attention returned to Sage, a hungry light filled his dark eyes. "You, me, a snowstorm, and this fireplace."

Sage's breathing hitched as he thought about how that could turn out. "It's possible," he murmured breathily. "We get plenty of snow up here in the winter."

"Mmm, then we'll definitely keep an eye on the weather up here every winter and plan accordingly," Germaine told him with a wink.

Laughing, Sage grinned at his mate. "You know, most people plan to avoid snowstorms."

At his teasing, Germaine tugged him close and wrapped

his arms around him. "Well, we're definitely not most people."

Sage lifted his arms and wrapped them around Germaine's shoulders. "No." Rising onto his toes, he pressed his body against his lover, knowing he would keep him steady. "We're definitely not."

Germaine took his invitation, dipped his head, and sealed his mouth over Sage's. Opening immediately, he welcomed his snake shifter's tongue. Even after eating several cinnamon bears as dessert after their trip to the deli, he still tasted of deep masculine goodness.

At first, Sage had thought Germaine would change their plans and take him right to his cabin. To his pleasure, his mate had refused to allow some asshole's actions to impact them . . . much. They had been joined by Austin and Petre.

Sage hadn't even realized the lion shifter swung both ways, but he'd been very interested in learning about all-male fated mates. He'd even told the other man that he was welcome to visit him once he moved. After all, if he found a fated mate in Savannah, maybe Petre would, too. While he had never considered the lion shifter a buddy, Sage had a funny idea that he was making a great new friend.

When Germaine broke their kiss, he rested his forehead against Sage's own. "Your mind is drifting, my mate." His tone was soft without a hint of accusation. "Are you okay?"

"I guess I'm just feeling a little overwhelmed, Gere," Sage admitted. "My brain won't shut down. It keeps going over all the sudden changes in my life." Rubbing Germaine's neck, Sage whispered, "Sorry."

Germaine hummed as he pecked another gentle, lingering kiss to Sage's lips. "Don't apologize," he countered. "I bet you're overwhelmed. There's nothing wrong with that." Lifting his head, Germaine squeezed his waist. "Will you show me to your shower? Let's get out of these dirty clothes. We'll get clean, get dirty" — he waggled his eyebrows playfully — "then get clean again."

Sage chuckled as he nodded, his blood heating at Germaine's innuendo. "I can get behind that." He reached around and palmed his mate's ass. Then Sage reached between them and cupped his mate's crotch, pleased to feel it hardening under his touch. "Or in front of it."

Germaine groaned and bucked his hips. "My mate always has so many fantastic ideas." Even as he thrust into Sage's hold a second time, he said around panting breaths, "Yeah, let's go."

Laughing, Sage let go of Germaine's groin, gratified to hear his mate's needy groan. "I suppose I could lower your fly and lead you around by the dick," he teased.

To Sage's surprise, Germaine's eyes dilated so the pupil nearly beat out the deep brown of his iris. "Oh, fuck. I would so let you."

Sage sucked in a harsh breath as his blood coursed hot through his veins. His own cock throbbed at the idea, twitching behind his slacks. Looking down, he saw they were both tenting their pants in obvious arousal.

"I-I know that I could use a little relief," Sage murmured huskily, reaching for Germaine's fly. "Could you?"

"Hell, yeah, I could," Germaine replied breathily.

Needing to see, to touch, once more, Sage popped the button on Germaine's dress pants. He slid his palm into his mate's fly, cupping his shifter's length. Protecting his lover's smooth flesh, Sage lowered the zipper.

Just as it always seemed to happen when Sage spotted Germaine's cock, his mouth began to water. There was something about his mate's foot-long that sent his desires into overdrive. Sage wanted to lick him like a lollipop before sucking him until Germaine panted his name. If he rolled his lover's sensitive orbs just right, pre-cum would dribble into his mouth, coating his taste buds with his mate's lightly salty tasty goodness.

Delicious.

"Stop looking at me like that or we won't make it to the shower," Germaine warned, growling low in his throat.

"Oh?" Sage peered at Germaine from beneath his lashes. Putting a challenge into his voice, he asked, "And what exactly would happen if I didn't?"

Germaine narrowed his eyes, his grip on Sage's waist tightening with one hand. With his other, he popped the button of Sage's slacks. "Well." He lowered the zipper just enough to reveal Sage's drooling cock head. Then he began massaging his frenulum, sending shockwaves of pleasure down his staff. "I'd turn you to face the fireplace, grab the lube out of my pocket, and shove a couple fingers up your ass."

Sage sucked in a harsh breath as his brain began to fuzz out. "Th-That doesn't s-sound bad." As he spoke, Sage glanced toward the fireplace, then sidled a step toward it.

"Oh, it wouldn't be," Germaine assured, moving with him, giving in to the way Sage tugged on his erection. "But that wouldn't be all that I'd do."

While Germaine growled his warning, Sage didn't care. He wanted to experience exactly what was rattling around in his mate's brain—every time. Squeezing Germaine's dick tighter, Sage drew his lover ever closer to the fireplace.

"You're playing with fire," Germaine warned even as he continued to slide his fingers around Sage's flared head, then along the fringe of his cap. Finally, he returned to his frenulum and pressed.

Sparks shot straight to Sage's balls, and he whined, going up on his tip-toes. His balls began to tighten as the tingles settled in them. He felt the zing tickle the base of his spine, and he knew his orgasm was just around the corner.

Just a little more.

Sage rocked his hips, searching.

Germaine chuckled huskily as he eased the pressure.

Sage would forever deny the groan of dismay that escaped him.

"Not yet, my mate," Germaine told him. "Not until I'm buried so far up your ass you'll taste me in the back of your throat."

Moaning, Sage swallowed as if he already could.

"Turn around and step up," Germaine ordered on a growl.

It took more self-control than Sage thought he had to peel his fingers off of Germaine's exquisite erection, but he managed it. He turned and faced his fireplace. Feeling Germaine's hands return to his hips, he obeyed the man's urgings when it was obvious he wanted him to step up on the hearth, adding six inches to his height.

"Just about perfect," Germaine crooned. "Now grab the mantel, my mate. Both hands."

Trembling in anticipation, Sage obeyed, even though he really wanted to grab his cock for stimulus.

"Just need one more thing."

"Wh-What's that," Sage asked breathily.

"This."

Then Germaine gripped the back waistband of Sage's slacks and yanked. The fabric rent, the sound echoing in the quiet room. Sage sucked in a surprised gasp as cool air hit his ass, his pants falling halfway down his thighs.

"Perfect," Germaine crooned as he cupped Sage's ass cheeks. "Just perfect." One hand disappeared. Fabric rustled. Then Germaine murmured against his ear. "Here come my fingers."

Without any other warning, Germaine pressed damp fingers to Sage's hole . . . and thrust. Two long, slender digits breached him, going deep. The delicious stretch sent a burning tingle up his chute, and his cock twitched and oozed.

Moaning his delight, Sage gripped the mantel tighter. He

thrust out his ass, searching for more. His mate didn't disappoint.

"That's the way, Sage," Germaine rumbled gruffly. "Show me how much you like any part of me in you. Fuck yourself on my fingers."

Sage wouldn't have been able to stop his body's need even if he'd tried. His hips stuttered, and he gave up trying to resist. He jerked forward, then thrust back again . . . and again . . . and again.

With each move, Germaine glanced oh-so-slightly against Sage's prostate. It was maddening and amazing and sent blood roaring in his ears in the best and worst ways. His balls were heavy and full, but with his hands on the mantel and Germaine's fingers avoiding his pleasure gland, Sage just couldn't get there.

"Pleeeeeease," Sage begged as he continued to rut spastically.

"Please what?" Germaine rumbled into his ear. His back pressed against Sage's, and he could feel the man's heat even through their shirts. "Tell me what you need."

Sage felt Germaine's cock bump his back leg, and he moaned at the dampness, telling him his mate leaked for him. "Your cock," he panted. "I need your cock."

"How do you need it?" Germaine demanded. "How do you need my cock?"

"In my ass." Sage dug his nails into the wood, arching his back a bit more. "Deep in my ass."

Germaine's growling moan was music to Sage's ears. "Anything for you, my mate," he stated as he pulled his fingers free. "Push out."

Then Sage felt Germaine's flared head against his opening, and he obeyed. His lover's long, slender rod sank deep into his body — in and in and in. Sage welcomed the stretch, the burn, the sensation of being filled by the other half of his soul.

When Germaine's pubic hairs pressed into Sage's ass crack, his mate's balls nuzzling against his own, his lover stilled. He blanketed Sage—their bodies flush from thigh to shoulder. With one arm wrapped around Sage's torso and the other around his waist, Germaine held still, coupled deeply.

"Sage," Germaine groaned into his ear. "Feel so perfect." He nuzzled his lips along Sage's neck, licking, kissing, and nipping. "Could stay just like this forever."

"Gere," Sage murmured, tipping his head back to rest it on Germaine's shoulder. "I—"

Germaine licked at his earlobe. "I know what you need," he countered when Sage ran out of words. "Come for me. Just like this."

Then Germaine began the tiniest of ruts that Sage had ever felt. His long erection teased at his inner walls as well as his prostate. Fire burst through his rectum, igniting him from the inside out in the best heat possible.

"Gere," Sage mumbled again, trembling in his mate's hold. "So . . . so . . . so . . . oh!"

Sage's body erupted. His balls pulled tight, and his orgasm slammed into him. As heady endorphins sent him soaring, he felt Germaine's continued micro-ruts, keeping him stimulated and sending him even higher.

Shuddering and jerking in Germaine's firm hold, Sage moaned, calling his mate's name. He rolled his head on his lover's shoulder as his cock pulsed untouched. Burst after burst of sensation rocked through him.

"Gorgeous," Germaine rumbled right before his teeth sank into Sage's neck.

Screaming in ecstasy, Sage flew on the wings of a second orgasm, which somehow seemed even more intense.

When Sage felt his senses returning, he felt wrung out and sated in a way he never could have imagined. He'd dropped his arms to his sides at some point, too exhausted and bliss-drunk to keep them up any longer. He rested all his weight on Germaine, who still stood behind him, clutching him in a tight hold.

He was also still impaled on his mate's very hard erection.

Confused, Sage tipped his head to peer at Germaine's profile. His mate's eyes were closed, and a smile curved his lips. He sported an expression of pure delight, which confused Sage.

"Gere?" Sage began tentatively.

"Yeah, babe?" Germaine even sounded content.

Sage lifted one hand and teased his fingertips along Germaine's forearm. At the same time, he clenched and released on his mate's cock. He watched Germaine's smile widen and heard his hum of appreciation.

"Yeah, that feels so good, babe," Germaine muttered. "Do it again."

Obeying, Sage reached back with his other hand and gripped Germaine's hip. "Should I keep going, um, until you come?"

Finally, Germaine cracked open an eyelid and met his gaze. "I came, Sage," he told him, confusing him further. Grinning, he chuckled. Germaine turned his head and pressed a kiss to the corner of Sage's mouth. "I told you I could stay in you just like this forever."

Nodding, Sage wondered, "Is that why you like to fall asleep half-hard in my ass?"

Germaine winked. "Yep." His smile faded a little. "Does it bother you?" Even as he asked, he didn't pull out or explain why he still sported a hard-on.

"Not at all," Sage replied honestly.

Before Germaine, he'd always considered himself a switch, but with his mate, he loved feeling him deep in his chute . . . a lot. Fortunately, Germaine urged him to fuck him often, too—just not before they fell asleep.

"I'm just confused as to why you're still hard," Sage admitted.

Laughing softly, Germaine lowered one hand and wrapped it around Sage's penis. "Because touching you and staying in your sweet body does it for me, Sage." He began stroking Sage's overly sensitive dick, stimulating him slowly so as not to hurt him. "Now, let's get this nice and hard so you can fuck me in the shower."

With his blood swiftly pooling back in his cock, Sage shuddered in Germaine's grip. "Yes, please."

"Anything for you, my mate," Germaine crooned into his ear while fingering his crown, teasing at his slit. "Can't wait for you to fill me with your cream. It feels so good warming my insides."

Just as Germaine's blunt words always did, Sage felt his blood heat and his prick quickly responded.

"Now, my mate."

Chuckling, Germaine rumbled, "So demanding. Always topping from the bottom."

While Sage knew that was true, that didn't stop Germaine from tormenting him for another good ten minutes before sliding out of him and allowing Sage to lead him to the shower.

Chapter Twelve

Germaine and Sage were lounging on the sofa, wrapped up in a quilt and each other while watching TV, when a knock sounded on the door. Glancing at the clock on the mantel, he saw that it was a little after four in the afternoon. He knew Dakota and the others were scheduled to drop by at six with dinner, so it wasn't them.

Sage shrugged as he shoved the blanket off of him. "Grab some sweats for me," he requested. "Second drawer on the left."

"You better not answer the door in the buff," Germaine grumbled, scowling at his mate even as he hurried from the room.

He heard Sage laugh as he called, "I won't."

As Germaine grabbed a pair of sweats from his travel bag, which he'd left on a chair in the bedroom after their shared shower, he heard Sage call, "Who is it?"

Germaine didn't hear the response as he donned his sweats. After grabbing a t-shirt, just in case, he crossed to Sage's dresser. He opened the drawer Sage had indicated and found his mate's sweatpants. It took a couple of more opening and closing of drawers to find shirts.

By the time Germaine located them, Sage was hurrying into the room. His expression appeared troubled as he grabbed his sweats and yanked them on. While he took his shirt from Germaine's hand, he didn't put it on.

"Who is it?" Germaine asked as he followed Sage back to the front of the cabin.

"Meribeth."

Germaine felt his brows shoot up as he froze halfway across the living room. "The alpha's daughter?"

Sage nodded as he unlocked the front door's deadbolt, then the knob. As he peeked around the door, swinging it open a little, he greeted, "Hey, Meribeth. Sorry about the wait." Sage seemed to be looking behind her even as he swung the door wider. "Come on it."

Seeing the skittish expression on the face of the young woman who entered, Germaine settled on the arm of Sage's sofa. He did his best to appear non-threatening. Smiling, he dipped his head in greeting as he cataloged the lion shifter's features.

Meribeth stood about five-foot-eight—a good height for a female lion shifter—with a willowy and strong frame. She had long, dark-blonde hair, which she'd tied in a thick braid that ran over her right shoulder. Her honey-brown eyes appeared troubled, and she twisted her fingers together before her.

"Thank you for letting me interrupt, Sage," Meribeth murmured, glancing between them. She stood in the foyer, shifting from foot to foot nervously.

Either she didn't have much experience with men, or she didn't have experience with seeing people on her own.

"Sure, Meribeth," Sage replied soothingly. "Happy to help anytime." He backed away from her as he pulled on his shirt. Once his head popped out, he smiled at her and used his chin to indicate Germaine while threading his arms through the appropriate holes. "This is Germaine Messalla, my mate."

Germaine smiled at Meribeth. "Nice to meet you," he stated. He didn't offer her his hand, since she looked too nervous to take it. "Can I get you a drink? Coffee? Tea?"

Meribeth shook her head as she whispered, "Nice to meet you, too." Then she immediately asked, "Is it true that you're fated mates?"

Sage grinned widely. "It is." He moved toward Germaine, offering Meribeth more space, which seemed to cause her to relax a little, the tension in her neck and shoulders loosening. "I gotta admit, I was pretty blindsided when I met Germaine, but he helped me understand." Sage rested his hand on Germaine's shoulder as he pressed his hip against his thigh. "Did you, uh . . ." Sage seemed to stall out, clearly uncertain where to go with his question.

Making an educated guess, Germaine asked, "Is there someone you've met that you think might be your mate?" He hesitated, remembering Sage's suspicions about her, before adding, "A female someone?"

Snapping her head up, Meribeth stared at them wide-eyed. She quickly shook her head, her cheeks pinking darkly. Wrapping her arms around her torso, she peered around the large front room, her focus seeming to skitter over everything.

"N-No. No." Meribeth's brows furrowed. "I just . . ." She paused again, obviously struggling.

Deciding a subject change might be in order, Germaine stated, "If you don't mind my asking, Meribeth, but where did you learn that Germaine and I were fated mates?"

Meribeth's light-pink lips curved in a grimace. "It's going through the pride like wildfire," she revealed. Peering at them through her lashes, she admitted, "Gwendolyn had just shown up after breakfast, and you all were in the front room with Father, and we both overheard what you all were talking about." Lowering her gaze to the floor, Meribeth admitted, "At first, we didn't believe it because how could Dad be wrong. You know? Then a couple of pride-members starting telling how you and Germaine were holding hands in town, and they saw Petre and some other huge guy having lunch with you at the deli." Meribeth sucked in a sharp breath, then started rambling again. "Then there was that blond-haired guy who tried to run you down with his car, so someone must have been angry that the secret was out. Plus, Gwendolyn and I stopped at Petre's and questioned him, and he explained a few things, too. After that—" She snapped her mouth shut and bit into her lower lip as her honey-brown eyes took on a tell-tale gleam that she was trying to control her emotions.

Sage pushed off from his position. "Meribeth, what happened?" he purred softly, moving toward her. "What's wrong?"

While Germaine did wonder that, he was more curious about something else she'd said. What blond-haired man? Who had seen him, and did they know anything else about him?

Before any questions could be answered, the crunch of gravel under tires reached them in the cabin. Sage frowned as he stepped left and peered through the curtain. Before Germaine could caution Sage, his mate grabbed the knob and pulled open the door.

Germaine rose from the sofa's arm and headed toward Sage. Before he could reach him, a slender, auburn-haired man came barreling across the yard. He slammed into Sage and clung.

By the time Germaine reached Sage, he'd realized the guy wasn't attacking him. Instead, between his shaking shoulders, the hiccupping noises he was making, and the salty scent of tears filling the air, Germaine realized the guy was, well, bawling.

Sage, on the other hand, was rubbing his hands up and down the man's back, making shushing and soothing noises. His mate peered over the guy's shoulder and mouthed a word. It took Germaine a second, coupled with the scent of fox shifter, for him to realize that the crying man in his mate's arms had to be Randy.

"M-Maybe I should g-go," Meribeth whispered from Germaine's left. "I'm so sorry to interrupt."

"No, wait," Germaine murmured, touching her shoulder lightly. She flinched a little, so he didn't linger. Instead, he told her, "I think maybe we could all use some tea. Will you help me?"

Meribeth hesitated, then nodded. "Okay."

Germaine reached beyond Sage and urged the pair over a step so he could close and lock the door. Then he led the way into Sage's kitchen, giving his mate a moment with his friend. Never would he have thought he would willingly leave his mate with an ex-lover, but something in him knew the other man was absolutely no threat to his bond with Sage.

Once in the kitchen, Germaine stared around the space. "Uhhh, I actually have no idea where anything is," he admitted with a wry smile. "Or if he even has tea." Rubbing the back of his neck, Germaine told her, "This is my first time here."

Cocking her head, Meribeth asked, "It happens that fast?"

Germaine nodded. "For paranormals, yes. We meet our fated mate and will do anything to cement our bond and spend the rest of our lives with that special someone." Smiling at her confused expression, Germaine added, "That person is the other half of your soul, Meribeth. Once you meet him or her, you'll totally understand."

Then Germaine began opening and closing cupboards, checking out the contents. He took the time to let her process what he'd said. After a few seconds, she joined him in their search.

"You guys were right, you know," Meribeth whispered as they searched. "I was dating Gwendolyn, in secret, and when she found out fated mates are real, well—" She paused and sighed. "She thought maybe we should start going to clubs together to start looking." With her face flushing, Meribeth mumbled, "How can I watch the woman I've been intimate with search for someone else?"

Germaine paused and crossed the room to Meribeth. Gently, he rested his hand on her shoulder. "That's a difficult request she's making of you," he told her. "I'll be honest. I've never been in a relationship, so I'm not certain I can give you the right advice, but please know, if you ever need anyone to talk to, me and Sage are just a phone call away."

Meribeth's eyes gleamed a little as she nodded. "Thank you."

After an encouraging smile, Germaine released her.

Eventually, Germaine found a teapot, a canister with an assortment of individually wrapped tea bags, and a bottle of whiskey. It wasn't as high-end as what Mycroft always had on hand, but it wasn't cheap stuff either. Germaine made a mental note to question his mate about his choice as he put water on to boil.

"What's with the whiskey?" Meribeth asked as she pulled down mugs for them all.

Germaine leaned his butt against the counter and crossed his arms over his bare chest. "Well, that's Randy out there." He kept his voice quiet, hoping to avoid disturbing his mate. His sensitive hearing allowed him to make out soft words, but not what they were. "He's been in a relationship for a long time with another shifter named Cain." With a shrug, he murmured, "Considering he's here crying into Sage's t-shirt after finding out about fated mates a few days ago, there could be problems." Germaine tipped his chin toward the whiskey. "A little liquid fortification to help everyone as we talk, if we so choose." It was then he realized he wasn't completely certain how old Meribeth was. Arching a brow and giving her a teasing look, he asked, "You twenty-one?"

A shadow of a smile teased around the pretty young

woman's lips. "Yes. I'm over twenty-one. Twenty-seven, actually."

"Ah, you are young," Germaine commented. Tapping his chest, he revealed, "Two hundred and forty-three."

Meribeth's eyes widened. "And you're just now finding your mate?"

Germaine nodded. "Some people never find their fated mate. That's why it's considered such a gift by Fate."

Upon hearing a choked noise from the doorway, Germaine spotted Randy there. His face was tear-streaked, and he had his lower lip caught between his teeth. His nostrils flared. For all the world, he looked as if he were struggling to keep from bursting into tears once more.

Sage rubbed Randy's back, his expression pained.

Just then, the whistle on the kettle blew.

Germaine hurried and turned off the burner. Returning to the counter, he began pouring the steaming water into the mugs. "Does everyone want to choose a tea bag?" he urged. Trying to lighten the mood, Germaine winked the guys' way and asked, "Whiskey or no?"

Within a few minutes, everyone had chosen tea, and everyone had added a little whiskey. They returned to the living room, where Germaine and Sage sat together. Meribeth curled up on the floor near the fireplace—which Sage had started before they'd turned on the TV, even though it wasn't needed. Randy settled on a recliner with a sigh.

After Sage muted the TV, Randy sighed again. "Cain met his mate," Randy mumbled, staring into his drink. "I got home this afternoon, and he was sitting at the dining room table. I'd never seen the shell-shocked look on his face before, so I knew it was something . . . life-altering." Raising his gaze to meet theirs, Randy whispered, "We'd decided to stay together, but to start looking, and we would support each other even after we found them, but this guy is a human and a trucker, and he's only in town once every other week." With an expression of anguish, Randy whispered, "How could I make Cain wait two weeks? He even offered!" More tears slipped down Randy's cheeks. "I told him to go."

Germaine didn't know what to say. He'd always known his fated mate was out there, so he'd never been in a relationship. He could never imagine what Randy could be going through.

"I know this isn't what you want to hear," Sage murmured as he rose from his seat and crossed to him. Kneeling beside Randy, he rested his hand on his knee. "You did the right thing. The bigger thing." His smile appeared sad. "And I firmly believe Fate will bless you for it."

"She'll never get the chance."

Germaine whipped his head around and gaped at who he spotted. "Cranston?"

"That's right, you asshole. You and your fucking mate have ruined my life at Shifter Headquarters," the owl shifter claimed. "So I'm gonna kill you all before I disappear. Got plenty of friends who'll take me in."

"Who are you?" Sage demanded, although his voice quavered, probably due to the gun Cranston held in his right hand.

"He's Cranston Burgess," Germaine supplied. "He's Councilman Peregrine's aide. Let me guess. You're the one writing the reports and squelching any information about male fated mates."

"That's right," Cranston declared. "And if it wasn't for Sage showing up and revealing that packs and such in Peregrine's territory still didn't know faggot mates existed, no one would have been the wiser. So he's gonna die."

Cranston levered his gun at Sage, making Germaine damn near see red.

"Sage, when I take Cranston out, call Dakota," Germaine

ordered. "Got it?"

Even as Germaine saw Sage nod from the corner of his eye, Cranston laughed. "How do you expect to—"

Capitalizing on the distraction, Germaine shifted. As an enforcer, he changed damn fast—in seconds. Embracing his snake and his need to protect his mate, his snake emerged even faster.

Between one heartbeat and the next, Germaine took the form of his massive, twenty-four-foot anaconda. He heard several screams as well as the report of Cranston's gun. Then he wrapped his coils around Cranston, bringing the struggling shifter to the hardwood floor.

Germaine squeezed, rearing over their attacker. He heard the bones of the shifter creak, pleasing him. Opening his mouth, he hissed aggressively, relishing the way the scent of urine filled the air, telling him he'd made the owl shifter piss himself.

"Gere."

Turning his head, Germaine flicked out his tongue. He scented his mate and offered a low snarl of greeting.

"Dakota's on his way," Sage told him, easing closer. "You might want to loosen your hold before you kill him." As he spoke, he kicked the gun toward Randy, who was holding a pale-featured Meribeth in his arms. "He's out cold. We're all safe now."

Germaine turned his head and refocused on Cranston. He hissed his displeasure. The other shifter was indeed unconscious, but he really wanted to kill him anyway.

A deep voice ordered through the speaker on the phone in Sage's hand, "Germaine, relax your coils, at least a little. We're two minutes out." After a few seconds, the fellow enforcer added, "I have that pineapple pizza you love so much, but you don't get any if you kill him!"

Indecision filled him.

Pineapple pizza or the opportunity to kill the guy who threatened

107

my mate?

Both were so damn enticing.

Sage chuckled softly as he lightly skimmed his palm over Germaine's head. "I won't hold it against you if you take the pizza," he teased with a smirk. "Even if I think pineapple on a pizza is damn disgusting."

Hissing, scandalized, Germaine relaxed his coils and eased away from the unconscious Cranston. He shifted in seconds and peered up at Sage from his knees. "You don't like pineapple on your pizza?" He couldn't believe what he was hearing. "How is that possible?"

Laughing, Sage shook his head. "Go get dressed, and I'll forgive you for your horrible taste in food."

Germaine growled under his breath, shaking his head as he rose to his feet. "How could Fate do this to me," he muttered as he stalked out of the room. "Doesn't like pineapple pizza and not even a thank you kiss for saving his ass."

"Germaine?" Sage called when he'd reached the doorway to the bedroom.

Pivoting, Germaine spotted Sage lunging at him. He easily caught his mate. When Sage slammed his mouth over his own, he quickly opened to him.

As Germaine headed into the bedroom, plundering Sage's mouth, he smiled against his mate's lips.

Yep. This is the kind of thank you I'll always welcome.

You may also enjoy the following from eXtasy Books Inc:

Interrogation Techniques
Charlie Richards

Excerpt

"You're coming, Del, and that's the end of it!"

Enforcer Delanrue Drudeson turned his head just enough to arch his left eyebrow as he pinned a side-eyed look on his youngest brother—Dakota.

"Seven," his brother continued. "And if you want that shit microbrew stuff you like, you can bring it your own damn self."

Delanrue—Del to his brothers and only his brothers—growled softly under his breath. It wasn't because he didn't want to go to his youngest brother's Christmas party. Actually, Del did.

Instead, Delanrue fought against curling his lip because he spotted Glade Kanston strutting down the corridor toward him. He found the other Shifter Council enforcer to be a piece of entitled, self-absorbed shit. Del had hoped he would be implicated in working with one of the rogue ex-councilmen, just so he could arrest him and never have to deal with him again.

Too bad that hadn't happened.

Glade was not only straight as an arrow with a stick up his ass, that stick meant he wasn't going to break any shifter laws, either.

Guess that's a good thing.

"I mean it," Dakota pressed, clearly misunderstanding his vocalization. He waved his finger under Del's nose while adding, "If you're not there by seven, I'll send —"

"I'll be there," Del stated in a low gruff voice. "Stop your bitchin'."

Del couldn't care less who Dakota thought he could send to get him to comply. If he didn't want to go somewhere, he wouldn't. The only time he did something he would rather not to was when he was ordered by the Shifter Council.

Seeing as Del loved his job as an enforcer and interrogator for the Shifter Council, that didn't happen too often.

"Good," Dakota replied, sounding smug. Then he must have spotted who actually held Del's attention, for he muttered, "Oh."

Del grunted, but left it at that, since by then, Glade had drawn close enough to be within earshot. Trying to avoid true interaction, he met the lion shifter's gaze and dipped his chin in the barest of nods. Then Del focused his attention down the hall past the man.

From the corner of his eye, Del saw that Dakota did much the same thing. Then his brother returned to their conversation, and Del knew it was a ploy to keep Glade from attempting to engage them. Especially since Del knew Dakota was already aware that he knew the information.

"Dane said he might be bringing a date," Dakota told him, a chuckle in his tone. "If he can convince the lady to join him, that is." With an open laugh, his brother added, "Guess our brother is having trouble convincing her that he's sincere."

"Probably because he's not," Del replied absently. Shaking his head, he thought about their middle brother's desire to date a human woman named Linda. "She's not his mate. I don't see why Dane is bothering. He can never reveal what we are to her, and he'll have to dump her eventually anyway."

Del had never understood why a shifter would date someone who was not only not a paranormal, but not their fated mate. There was no future there. Besides, even if they did decide to date a paranormal, Fate could place their mate in their path at any second.

Even though Del had warned his brothers of that very thing on many occasions, both of them had been in and out of many relationships over the nearly two centuries they'd lived. Del would sit back and watch, and when their liaison inevitably fell apart, he'd helped his brothers mend their hearts.

"Dane is dating some poor hapless woman?" Glade smirked, stopping to stand in their path. He even crossed his arms over his chest as if that would make him some immovable object. "I bet he hasn't even let the lady know he's a dick licker. Maybe I should swing by tonight and let her know."

Del twisted his lips into a scowl as he glared at Glade. "Watch your mouth, Enforcer Glade," he ordered. As the council's lead interrogator, in the intricate hierarchy within those working for the Shifter Council, Del's position topped the lion shifter. "Or someone on the council may hear about your slurs."

Glade tipped his chin up and attempted to look down his nose at Del and his brother. "I'm sure I wouldn't have anything to worry about. I work under Councilman Peregrine, after all," he stated, referring to an elk shifter who disagreed with homosexual matings. "He knows the true value of loyalty."

Councilman Georgio Peregrine's views had nearly caused him to lose his position, since he'd been backing other councilmen who were committing crimes against shifter-kind. When those crimes had come to light, the councilman had turned against them. That hadn't changed what he thought about gay matings, however. It just meant he was more subtle about where and when he voiced those views.

Evidently, he shares them with Glade.

Del knew better than to engage a bigot. Besides, he had places to be. He was in the middle of interrogating the last half dozen shifters who'd been captured when they'd taken down the now-deceased rogue ex-councilman Krakow.

Good riddance.

Taking a step to the left and forward, Del began rounding the idiot standing in the middle of the hall. He noticed Dakota doing the same to his right. He peered beyond the man, turning his thoughts to the upcoming interrogation he needed to do.

That morning, Del had picked the brains of two bear shifters and one tiger shifter. Then he'd stopped to have lunch with Dakota. His afternoon would consist of the last three men they'd found.

Finally, the dungeons would be empty . . . of those people anyway.

Del knew a few shifters had been brought in for other crimes, but they hadn't been a priority. The council wanted all the information they could on Krakow's contacts, so they'd focused on his associates. Unfortunately, the wolf shifter hadn't shared too much about his organization with his minions — probably because he thought they were beneath him.

I bet Pedro knows something, though.

Pedro Kenbrook had been Krakow's accountant for over a hundred years. He'd created false accounting information to hide his activities — payment for the sale of shifters as well as the money Krakow had paid to the mercenaries who captured them. Their cyber team had also uncovered files on the serums that the military was concocting by experimenting on shifters, although the formulas were incomplete.

Can't wait to make that guy crack.

They'd purposefully made Pedro wait until the end, allowing him to watch cell-mates disappear from around him.

"Hey, don't you walk away from me," Glade snapped, grabbing Del's upper arm. "I'm not done talking to you."

Del barely resisted rolling his eyes. With his thoughts on his duties, he'd nearly forgotten Glade was there. Pausing, he pinned the moronic lion with a cold gaze. "Not wise to put your hands on me," he stated, cutting a quick glance at where Glade had the audacity to touch him without permission.

Glade scoffed, although a hint of uncertainty crossed his features, but only for a second.

No sense of self-preservation.

"Like I said," Glade claimed. "You can't do anything to me. I'm Peregrine's favorite."

Del was damn tempted to sock the other shifter anyway. He couldn't give a shit that Glade thought he was untouchable. Seeing Dakota move to stand next to him and taking in his brother's angry expression, he knew the other male was way out-classed.

We'd wipe the floor with him.

That was exactly why Del resisted.

ABOUT THE AUTHOR

Charlie started writing fantasy when she was eight, and after stumbling onto her first erotic romance at age nineteen, she realized her true calling. She now focuses on writing gay erotic romance, normally of the paranormal variety, with heroes of all kinds. With the help and support of her husband, Charlie finally fulfilled one of her life-long goals . . . move to acreage with her horses. You can often find her curled up with her laptop and a cup of tea or glass of wine, creating her next adventure. Charlie enjoys exploring the mountains of her new Oregon home on horseback, 4-wheeler, or motorcycle.

She can be reached at ch.richards2010@yahoo.com

Or visit her at www.charlie-richards.com